ESSAYS
AND
FICTIONS

Tyrant Books
827 N Lamar Blvd
Oxford, MS 38655

www.NYTyrant.com

ISBN 978-0-9992186-4-8

Third Printing

Book design by Adam Robinson
Cover design by Brent Bates

ESSAYS  AND FICTIONS

Brad Phillips

TYRANT BOOKS
New York and Rome

For Cristine

That each new indignity defeats only the body,
pampering the spirit with obscure merit.

—Donald Newbury, final statement.
Executed February 5, 2015
Huntsville State Penitentiary

CONTENTS

OPHELIA

Modern flash drives are much smaller than Bic lighters. They can contain hours of perverse homemade pornography. I've lost many Bic lighters.

I SAT THERE CONVINCED THAT NO MATTER WHAT, I wouldn't leave. That for the first time in my life, I would be completely honest with a therapist. However, sitting in the waiting room, I noticed five things within the first ten seconds that would have made it reasonable for me to leave before even meeting the doctor. This was something I'd done multiple times in the past.

1. A fern was dying in the corner. The logic here is simple: if you can't even keep a houseplant healthy, how are you going to help me get healthy? Plants only require water and light. I require a whole lot more.
2. A framed Modigliani print was hanging on the wall. Modigliani is grossly overrated. There's a faux-moodiness to his palette, a lazy mannerist style that fuses Byzantine painting with El Greco. It is "just right for the therapist's office" and therefore exactly wrong, and cause to leave.
3. The print was hung crookedly. The reasoning here is similar to number one. Is it really that hard?
4. Carpeting. I don't imagine I need to elaborate.
5. This may seem like nothing but it's not: fluorescent lighting. This type of lighting is known to suck the essence out of the human soul. A flickering tube-shaped succubus. It's important to think about lighting.

Regardless, I stayed in the chair as I'd promised myself. I told myself that when my name got called I would walk into the office and take the seat offered me. I had also promised Audrey, my wife, that I would not treat being in therapy as material, as research with which to make art or write stories. I knew as soon as it came out of my mouth that it would be an impossible promise to keep.

Why have I never told the truth in therapy? For one, I don't think anyone does. When I hear people say, 'It was unimaginable,' I immediately think, well, these people have no idea what I can get up to imagining. Essentially I think I am too sick, medically and morally, for any therapist to find the empathy required to listen to what I have to say then offer me advice.

Honesty persistently eludes me like a scared child being followed by a white van with curtains on the windows. There is a horror in writing. There are things I won't write here knowing it will be read by people I love, who love me. My life is what I know best and can use as material most expertly, yet I don't want to hurt those in my life who may become that material by writing about them. There are writers who do it, maybe they just change a name and the color of a character's hair, but nobody's fooled. Those writers always seem to be lonely and hated, and I'm already doing well on both those fronts. I don't want to further secure my isolation by publishing things that expose, hurt or embarrass others, so I make up for that elision by doubling up on the amount of material that hurts, exposes and embarrasses me. It can be read as self-loathing, but that's not it.

Or, maybe it is and that's what I'm in therapy to find out.

My shortest relationship with a psychiatrist was in 1998. A few hours before the second session, I realized there was no way I was going to be able to get over his impossibly black, ill-fitting wig, so I left.

My longest was in Vancouver with Doctor D___ Fung. It lasted three years. At the time, my general practitioner was also named Doctor Fung, and my pharmacist was named Doctor Fung. I was locked inside of a Fung triangle. People on the West Coast put a lot of stock in the healing power of the triangle, but I can say that having experienced the Fung triangle, its only effect was that it made me sicker, sadder, angrier and more self-destructive.

I put up with psychiatrist Fung. From day one it was a put-up-with type scenario. He was smart, but there was a problem. Although he was Chinese, he'd been born in England and moved to Canada in his twenties. There should not have been a language problem, yet there was. I'm obnoxiously fastidious about language, particularly the way people speak, and I have very little patience for vocalized pauses such as *um* and *like*. Fung could compete on the international stage when it came to vocal filler. He also had a habit I'd never encountered before of confusing tenses in conversation. He'd say things like, "So I thought that you're saying you didn't want to drink, but I think you're saying that you actually do, and I thought what should we discuss about that?" I felt lost and confused by these sentences, and it was terribly hard not to point it out to him. That I didn't is strange, but it's likely because feeling intellectually superior to him allowed me to disregard any of his thoughts about me, as well as any advice he offered.

Once I fired him, I realized the reason I'd stayed with him for so long was because it took me an hour to get to his office, where I had an hour-long appointment, and an hour to get back. He got me away from my wife for three hours. And the chair in his office was much more comfortable than anything meant for sitting on in my home.

So I sat in the waiting room looking for reasons to leave and reminding myself that I wouldn't. Five minutes remained until my appointment. I like to come early to doctors appointments because I like to see what's happening in the world of contemporary magazines. The ones Dr. Morris had fanned out on the table offered me very little. I did learn, however, of a magazine devoted to collectors of pens, Pen Collector, and briefly thought the world was wonderful.

The door opened and a woman in her late forties came out. She had permed hair, a linen jacket, printed skirt; her eyes were puffy and swollen from crying. So, it's one of *these* offices, I thought. An office without a secondary exit. I liked secondary exits. The suffering needn't meet the suffering in the anteroom of suffering. In the past this would have been a reason to leave. Yet I prepared to stand up.

"Mr. Phillips, please, come in."

The truly gorgeous white male cannot be intimate with suffering, and at least a passing familiarity with personal suffering is a prerequisite for being a good therapist. This therapist was too good-looking. His hair looked like it had been cut and styled a certain way for his entire life. It looked like he snapped it off before bed and back on in the morning. His teeth were white as paper. There wasn't anything wrong with him. I comforted myself. I was at least an inch taller than him. For stupid prehistoric reasons, this was very important to me. But you will stay. You will go sit in his office. He led me in and directed me to the chair opposite his desk. Now was the time to employ my gift, my analysis of the analyst. I searched for signs that could justify my departure.

He sat at his desk. I sat in the chair, which supported my thoracic and lumbar spine in ways I hadn't previously known possible. I could see this relationship having legs. In the chair, under the spell of its empathetic support, I decided to take in my primary area of interest: the placement of framed degrees.

Ideally, a therapist should have their various degrees framed and exhibited—as he or she is entitled to that after so much study and expense—discreetly on a wall off to the side. A patient's eye should never be drawn in by rectangles of validation. Yet Dr. Morris, Dr. *Leslie* Morris, sat facing me with an array of degrees and certificates behind him, situated as to frame his face in the middle of them. One handsome man in a galaxy of authentication. Not threatening, yet not *unthreatening*.

My feet were anxious in their shoes. I wanted to get going. I consciously planted my feet on the floor.

On Dr. Morris' desk, facing him but visible to me if I angled myself obliquely and inconspicuously enough, I could see a small framed photograph depicting the doctor on some sort of yacht, his arm around the shoulder of an attractive younger woman in a white one-piece bathing suit. Is this a photo that elicits any sexual arousal in the doctor? I wondered. It would in me.

Canada is much like America, except, in all the ways America is garbage, Canada is delightful. Guns are very rare here, and I was shocked to see a small pistol hanging on the wall to the left of me. It didn't look antique or collectible. It seemed to possess more personal than historical significance, as if it was the gun Dr. Morris had used to kill the intruder who took his only daughter's life years ago. The gun and the degrees lent the office a slightly threatening ambience I enjoyed. Surprisingly, another check in the do-not-leave-this-office column.

I heard his voice and I heard my own, and I realized that this was perhaps a sign of my own mental illness: I'm able to hear myself socializing while having a complex internal experience about a completely different subject. I was discussing my longstanding opiate addiction, but not quite getting into the grimy stuff, instead focusing on my desire to stop taking Tylenol #1 with codeine. I have never been a lazy junky, except in this regard:

I've not once used the cold-water extraction method to tease out the codeine and discard the liver-damaging acetaminophen in the pills. There was a time in my mid-to-late twenties when I took upwards of forty of them in the morning, waited just long enough to feel myself start to get high, and then ate a little food so that I didn't get nauseous and throw up. Those days were long gone though. Now it was a less intense habit, and I mostly just took them out of fear of withdrawal. I told the doctor that I wanted to stop taking them.

Then, suddenly and uncharacteristically, I had to urinate. I asked Dr. Morris where the bathroom was and he told me to go out the way I came in. When I opened the door to the waiting room, I was confused when I saw the woman who I'd previously seen leaving the office sitting in a chair reading a magazine. There was also another woman: tall, elegant, grey hair, near sixty, wearing a red dress that was far too classy for therapy. Her hands were folded in her lap and she smiled at me as I passed.

While I sat on the toilet taking a piss, I thought that this was all inauspicious, the lack of separate passageways most therapists use to keep the patients from encountering each other. It seemed like some depressive key party or pre-orgy waiting room. Why was the woman who'd been in his office before me sitting in the waiting room as if she was up next? It was odd. The fact that it *was* so odd though made me view it as yet another check in the stay-with-this-therapist column. Shrinks are always so very much the same that any deviation from standard script or setting is interesting.

After pretending to wash my hands by turning the water on and off I returned to the waiting room. Now the two women were sitting next to each other, and they were laughing. The elegant woman in the red dress emphasized a point by touching the other woman's thigh; they giggled like they were sharing a secret. When I walked past them they both looked up at me and smiled. I smiled back, sort of. This certainly did not seem to be an anteroom of suffering. When I closed the door to Dr. Morris' office I heard another giggle, and he smiled. I returned to the kind and affectionate chair.

Dr. Morris asked me to pick up where I'd left off, and I heard myself telling him that there had been a point in my mid-thirties that had really depressed me, when I realized I was able to pour exactly twenty-four Tylenol #1's into my hand each time with one shake. I knew exactly how to manipulate the bottle, the weight and motion required, to give me twenty-four pills. At the time, that was the number of pills I could take without food and not get nauseous. It was a sad and unique skill to have developed, a skill developed solely by the grinding routine of addiction.

I told him of my first wife and the places I'd hide the empty bottles in our apartment, how she never once found them; how when she'd go to school I'd put them all, maybe a dozen or more, in a small shopping bag, then walk down the street to the subway, depositing one or two at a time in different public garbage cans. I didn't know why I did this. He nodded expertly. But you're not doing that now? he asked.

I told him no, because that was the truth. Here I was telling the truth, just as I'd promised myself. I told him I'd been trying to wean myself off for months now unsuccessfully. I'd get down to a reasonable amount, then have a flare-up of pain and take way too many. But I kept the bottle visible to my wife, which was why she kept reminding me to talk honestly with my doctor. I told the doctor I wanted to stop, but I was scared of withdrawal.

He started making sounds with his mouth that reminded me of words when I noticed that the photo on his desk, the one of him on a yacht embracing the lithe young body of a woman in a white bathing suit, had been moved forward and turned to face me directly. It was extraordinarily unnerving and bizarre. Why would he do that? I've been to a lot of doctors, experienced a lot of different therapeutic modalities, but this was entirely new to me. He knew from our phone consultation that I felt my sexuality was a mental illness. Was this meant to rattle me? If it were meant to disturb me, then surely he'd be looking at me, I thought. But he was talking to me about the roots of addiction while leaning back in his chair and looking up towards the ceiling. I tried to ignore it. I scanned the room for other things that might even out the columns in my mental checklist, but I was distracted. I tried to look past the photo and focus on him.

Then I saw it: a new photograph on the desk, in precisely the same place and position as where the other one had originally been. I feigned adjusting myself and tilted my head so I could see it. It was a framed snapshot of Dr. Leslie Morris, this time standing on what I recognized to be the Ponte Vecchio in Florence. He was wearing a white linen suit and had the head of yet another beautiful young woman tucked inside his strong bicep. She looked Eastern European and was wearing heavy eye makeup and not much more than a sheer orange dress, which I was pretty certain I could see her breasts through.

Dr. Morris sat forward in his chair now, staring directly into my eyes. It was very difficult to maintain eye contact, in part because I felt embarrassed, and in part because there were now two photographs which I found arousing sitting on his desk.

"I'm afraid our time's up, Brad," he said abruptly. "If today's good for you, then I can book you for the same time next week?"

We walked toward the door and he opened it for me, patting me lightly on the back. He told me he looked forward to seeing me again.

"Leslie, please come in," Dr. Morris told the woman in the waiting room. It was the woman who had left his office as I went in an hour prior. *Her name is also Leslie? And she's going back in for more therapy?* She quickly got up and tried to enter the office before I had fully left the doorway. The two of us got sort of stuck, bumping against each other like something from *The Three Stooges*. Dr. Morris used his strong masculine hands to help this other Leslie and me untangle ourselves, and I practically fell into the waiting room while she went back into his office. The door shut and I heard a giggle. I waited a moment. Nothing. Suddenly, there was one deep, painful, genderless sob. I went to the washroom and splashed water on my face then walked down the stairs to the street.

When I got to the bus stop, the elegant woman in the red dress was there, smoking a cigarette, still looking like she was about to go to the symphony. I had a cigarette in my mouth but realized my lighter must've fallen out in the chair in Dr. Morris' office, so I asked her for a light. She looked at me like she'd never seen me before then told me she didn't have one. I mentioned to her that she was smoking and she told me to fuck off. The bus came and I got on ahead of her. As it pulled away, I looked out the window and saw her still standing at the stop. She'd put a new cigarette in her mouth and was lighting it with a red Bic lighter.

I was looking forward to the second session with Dr. Morris, strictly due to the possibility of bizarreness or perversity, so I showed up ten minutes early. The same fern was dying, the same carpet was carpeted. I was not going to leave. He was television somehow. I looked through the fanned magazines and picked up a copy of Pen Collector, different from the one I'd seen my last appointment. As I brought it toward my lap another magazine fell out. It was Janus, Issue 59, a British magazine from the late 1970s and early 1980s devoted entirely to caning, spanking, flogging—anything else involving a woman's rear end being the locus of discipline.

The cover was beautiful, and reminded me of photos I'd taken myself. Those magazines, while pornographic, are not what that word brings to mind. Often there is no nudity other than women's asses, usually with their panties pulled down, but not missing. They cater to a very specific type of person and have a very specific narrative. The image on the cover of this issue was of a woman in a red slip. She was standing in a doorway, dramatically lit from behind, with her hands clasped in front of her and her face and eyes downcast. The perspective was that of the dominant, the sadist, the behavior-corrector. She had been called to the doorway to answer for her errors.

I was turned on. I got up and hid the magazine under the mat by the door, to take it with me when I left. *Who has a fetish magazine in their waiting room?* I thought. *Or who brings one in and hides it inside a copy of* Pen Collector? Some sadist had probably brought it with him and was jerking off in the waiting room, or getting himself ready to, only to be interrupted by the call of "Please, come in." It occurred to me that there was in fact no magazine, overt or hidden, that would not make sense in the waiting room of a psychotherapist.

The office door opened. "Mr. Phillips, please, come in."

There she was again: Leslie, the female patient. Her cheeks were red and her eye make-up had smeared in rivulets, black marks where tears moved the pigment. Suddenly, I saw Lazara in my head, a particular moment in a cottage in upstate New York years ago, and I remembered the other reason why a woman's eye makeup might smear and run. Lazara certainly hadn't been crying that afternoon in New Paltz. I took a good hard look at Leslie. She wasn't suffering. She was depleted. She was satisfied. For reasons I can't properly articulate, this was another check in Dr. Morris' favor.

I'd forgotten about the chair and fell into it like a fly into shit. Dr. Morris sat opposite me. He seemed to be doing that old sales trick of looking at the space between my eyes, not in my eyes, to let me think he was paying attention. That was fine with me. Pretending to pay attention was good enough. I was pretending to be in therapy. I heard the words, "How was your week, tell me what's going on with you?" and I heard myself answering him. "My week was fine, I feel overworked, I'm tired of living a life built on deadlines yet I'm terrified the deadlines will disappear."

I noticed one thing almost immediately. The space on the wall where the pistol had been now showcased another token of private significance: a photograph of Dr. Morris, this time in Japan, standing outside of a Shinto temple. He was wearing a white suit, white tie and white hat. His arm was around a striking woman with long dark hair. They were an extremely attractive couple. Dr. Morris kept talking and I kept replying, and then I realized who it was—it was the elegant woman from the week before who'd been giggling with Leslie and serving some unknown purpose in the office. Dr. Morris looked the same age in the photograph as he did sitting across from me, but the Elegant Woman looked much younger. Her hair hadn't yet turned grey; her face was much less angular, less drawn.

I looked around the room and saw a shape unfamiliar to me next to Dr. Morris' coffee cup. Amongst his pens and photos, staples and papers—the pistol. It seemed harmless enough, just sitting on his desk like that. The barrel wasn't pointed at either of us. I thought of movies; I searched my memory for knowledge of guns gleaned from them. Then I moved myself two inches to the right in my chair, ducked my head down slightly and looked directly into the chamber of the gun.

Five bullets were inside of it. One was missing.

There are innumerable reasons why a six-shot pistol might contain only five bullets. It didn't immediately mean one had been fired. I decided to stop thinking and focus on why I was there. We returned to discussing addiction, and my inability to stop taking Tylenol with codeine. It wasn't withdrawal I was afraid of, we concluded, because I'd done that, I had done the big withdrawal. So what was it then?

Dr. Morris offered an opinion I'd heard variations of before: I was self-destructive. Sure I was worried these pills might ruin my liver and cause an early death, but was there any chance that while that thought scared me, it was something I secretly desired? My answer was the same as it has always been: Yes.

I had never felt so strangely unlike myself, glued to a chair due to a vow of honesty. I suddenly became so bored I could barely stand it. He blathered, I blathered. Dr. Morris' eyes kept moving from one to another of the three photographs on his desk I couldn't see. Without looking up at me, Dr. Morris said he was afraid our time was up.

I was disappointed. That first session had been something else. As I stood up I became excited to see what the waiting room offered, but when he opened the door the only person in it was a teenage boy who had obviously come to therapy right after the humiliating experience of another day in high school.

"So, this time next week works for you?"

I said yes, because it did. Dr. Morris did not put his hand on my back this time. I was left to put my coat on and let myself out.

"Hi Tim, come in, come in. How are you today?" As I made my leave I looked back, only to see Dr. Morris and Tim close the door shut behind them, entering a room I saw as full of perversity and danger and things not meant for children. I felt strangely afraid for Tim. Were he to see the photograph of Dr. Morris in Japan, would he understand? Would he know imagery like that was not meant for the eyes of someone so young? I didn't worry about the gun. It was the photographs, those displayed and those hidden, that seemed to pose the most danger.

I didn't know what to expect of the third appointment. On the subway heading there I thought of Tim. Then I thought, Fuck Tim. I didn't want to see Tim. I wanted to see Leslie or the

Elegant Woman. I wanted to see them both. I wanted to see them both covered in canola oil and the office itself completely coated in rubber sheeting.

I also wanted to see Dr. Morris. I'd become fascinated with him. His photographs, his handgun, his inscrutability, his women. I wasn't thinking too much about my own problems or what I would say.

I got off the streetcar where I'd gotten off the previous two times. The neighborhood seemed eerily deserted, as cities often can mid-afternoon. I jaywalked across the street. There were no cars coming in either direction. I realized I'd actually been the only person on the streetcar, save the driver, then I thought back further and couldn't recall anyone else being on my subway car either. I stood outside Dr. Morris' office and smoked a cigarette. I thought of therapy scenes from films and wished that I could smoke inside while I talked about my problems. After around forty minutes with a shrink I always got distracted and started craving a cigarette.

I noticed the two businesses adjacent to the building Dr. Morris' office was in. To the left was a florist. To the right was a storefront with black curtains behind the window; through a small slit I could see that the interior was lit by neon lights. A small sliver of lurid red like a knife wound in the black screen. There was no sign above the window. I walked across the street toward it and looked at the door. In small ornate letters above a numerical keypad was the word *Ophelia*. No information about hours, no bell. Just an industrial looking doorknob and the numerical keypad.

Ophelia reminded me of something.

I flicked my cigarette butt onto the still empty sidewalk, crossed the street, then began the walk upstairs to Dr. Morris' office. I was excited. I was apprehensive. I didn't want to be let down.

When I got into the waiting room, there she was: the Elegant Woman, sitting this time in a low-cut black cocktail dress that revealed much of her breastbone, intimating to the right and left small breasts unsupported by underwear. She was also wearing stockings with a seam up the back. It would have been logical to think she was in a sort of sexy mourning, had it not been for her blinding patent red leather high heels. She looked up at me and smiled. I was surprised, considering our last encounter, so I smiled back.

I noticed she was reading the issue of *Janus*, Number 59, that I'd tucked under the mat last session and forgotten to take home. I saw the cover again, the woman in the red satin number standing in a submissive pose I found compelling, and was reminded of what the Elegant Woman had been wearing the first time I saw her in the office. Was what I had mistaken for a classy red dress really something meant to be worn *under* a dress? When I saw her that first time hadn't she had her hands folded demurely in her lap?

"Mr. Phillips, I was doing a bit of tidying up. It looks like you forgot this magazine that you hid under the mat."

How did she know my name? How did she know I'd secreted it for myself? How did she know what my intentions had been? I quickly scanned the room for cameras, but saw none.

"I don't know what you're taking about," was all I could come up with.

"Why don't you sit down?"

I took off my jacket and held it then went to sit as she'd suggested. I glanced at the fern, an insult to botany and nature itself at that point. This woman spooked me. I didn't want the conversation to continue. I went to sit by the wall opposite her but there was a small puddle of water in the seat.

"Leaky ceiling," she said.

I looked up. There was no visible leak in the ceiling. If

anything the room felt unusually dry. The two chairs adjacent to the one I'd tried to sit in both had small puddles on them too.

"Come on, Mr. Phillips."

I looked at all the chairs that weren't near her. They all had small puddles of water on them.

"You didn't do a very good job of tidying up, did you?"

I realized that the only dry seat in the office was the one next to the Elegant Woman, and the fabric my jacket was made of couldn't sponge up a puddle, so I hesitantly sat in it.

"That's not so bad, is it? I'm just reading, I won't bother you."

I sat next to her and folded my jacket in my lap, burying my hands beneath it. I realized that it might look like I was touching my dick, so I put my hands on top of my jacket instead. She kept flipping through the magazine. It was difficult not to look over and check out what she was looking at. Occasionally she'd quietly say "Ooh" or "Oh my." It was sexual, but confusingly so. I just wanted to be called into the office.

"Why didn't you take the magazine home?" she asked me. "What is it you're really here for anyway, Brad?"

I looked over and saw an image of a schoolgirl standing in a corner with her hands on her head while a female headmistress loomed behind her holding a cane. The Elegant Woman looked over at me before I could take my eyes off the page and I accidentally met her gaze. She opened her mouth slightly and a small portion of her tongue moisturized her bottom lip. She returned to looking at the magazine.

That familiar giggle sounded out from Dr. Morris' office and my body relaxed. Then the door opened. The female Leslie stood in the doorway holding a box. She was wearing a trench coat with the belt wrapped loosely enough around it that I could see she had nothing else on but stockings, a garter belt and a black brassiere. Her eyes were puffy as always, damp, but this time with unmistakable sadness. She looked directly at me and said, "Mr. Phillips, you may come in now."

The Elegant Woman put the magazine down and rose to her feet while Leslie walked toward her. She put the box on the floor so that they could embrace. They looked like high-end escorts at a funeral for a high-end escort. I just wanted to be back in the absurdly comfortable chair, free of their vaguely menacing and ambiguous sexuality, never mind the questions and inexplicable knowledge of the Elegant Woman. I stood there frozen for a moment and watched as Leslie handed off the box to the elegant woman. They held hands and began to leave. I heard the sound of their impractical shoes on the stairs.

The office was empty. No Dr. Morris. I let the chair embrace me as I waited. Maybe he was in the bathroom. But if he'd gone to the bathroom I would have seen him traversing the waiting room, no? The women had spooked me more than I'd realized. I fished a Clonazepam out of my pants pocket and swallowed it dry. I called out the doctor's name and was greeted by silence. The gun was back up on the wall. The desk had three photographs on it again, all facing the empty chair my therapist was supposed to be sitting in. I got up and walked over to the handgun. When I looked in the chamber I saw it was holding six bullets. I walked behind his desk and looked at the wall of validation that bothered me so much, but when I looked closer I saw that all the certificates and diplomas—undergrad at the University of Toronto, master's at Columbia, doctorate at Yale—were just photocopies, facsimiles put together in Photoshop. There were also degrees from obscure schools in Hypnotherapy and Behavioral Activation.

On his desk, I saw a file with my name on it. I sat down and opened it. Inside were photographs of me sitting in the waiting room, as well as caricatures of my face drawn impressively in pencil, my home address, my social security number and the details of my two credit cards. I took the file and folded it in half to take with me.

20

I remembered the framed photos that had so enraptured me at the same moment my eyes registered them. One on the left, one dead center, one on the right. I looked at the left one first. There was Dr. Morris, wearing a casual summer suit, beige, maybe linen. He was standing in the middle of what looked like a Japanese airport; his right arm hung over Leslie's shoulder, whose perm appeared bigger. She was wearing purple lipstick and a fur coat. While he was smiling, she seemed to be looking at something troubling off to the left. The photo in the middle showed Dr. Morris again, this time in a bathing suit, standing on a pristine beach, the ocean behind him. His arm was around the Elegant Woman, who was wearing an enormous floppy hat. She looked even younger than she had in the earlier photo; he looked the same age as always. Dr. Morris was smiling, and the Elegant Woman, though her eyes were barely visible within the shadow of her hat, seemed to be looking down at the sand. Then I looked at the photo on the right and began to shake uncontrollably.

In the third photo, Leslie and the Elegant Woman sat on either side of a man with their arms draped over his shoulder, their other hands in his lap. The man in the middle was me. I was wearing a sweater I had worn the week between my first and second visit, an old sweatshirt from the Universidad de Salamanca. The women were both smiling. I was staring somewhat apprehensively at something ahead of me. In the far distance of the photograph I saw a mirror. I picked the photo up and held it closer. Barely reflected but still legible I saw the word Ophelia in reverse, tinted neon red. I took the photo and my file and went and sat in the comfortable chair.

I took out a cigarette and lit it, staring at nothing, unsure of what I was thinking. I looked at the photograph and my file again. I ashed my cigarette on the carpet. Then I saw and reached for a large ornate Africanesque clay pot—the staple of any therapist who wants you to know he's cultured—and pulled it off the shelf. I put it on the floor in front of me and continued to smoke, as I used my lighter to set my file on fire. First, I lit the edge of the cardboard, then I tilted the file so that the flames attached themselves to all of the paper within, and I deposited it in the bowl.

I took the photo of myself out of the frame and lay it on top of the burning file. I watched the image of myself curl and ripple then turn to smoke and begin to rise out of the bowl. Small black embers floated gracefully then vanished. When I finished my cigarette I put it in the bowl and sat there until everything had burned away.

I was half expecting Tim to be in the waiting room—or worse, them—but there was nobody. I walked down the stairs quickly. Looking at Ophelia across the street, the window showed nothing but blackness. The street was full of people now and I walked to the bus stop. The first bus that came was too full for me to get on, so I hailed a cab. I got in and gave the driver my address. I leaned my head against the window and kept seeing that photograph in my mind. The files bothered me less, even though the information inside of them could potentially be much more harmful. It was seeing myself somewhere, with no memory of having been there that really fucked with me. I thought about looking up Ophelia in the phone book or online when I got home, but I decided that I should never look it up, never try to find it. I should forget it.

That evening at home I was particularly quiet. Lazara made dinner while I washed dishes. She asked me how my appointment went, and I said it was okay. She asked me if I was going to go keep going, and I told her yes, I was. Unmistakably, this was a lie, and I knew from my experience with lying that it would either be fine, or that it would end horribly. There could be no safe and cozy middle. I told her that I still was going to continue to be honest, no matter how difficult I found it.

SUICIDAL REALISM

"When I die fuck it I wanna go to hell, cause I'm a piece of shit it ain't hard to fucking tell"

—Notorious B.I.G.

1.

Here is a made up story, here is playing pretend.

Imagine that I'm writing this after putting 200 milligrams of Morphine up my right nostril, which was horrific but necessary as the left one is a latticework of scabs and narco-mucous. It did burn. The good kind of burn. I mixed in 2 milligrams of Clonazepam—making three gigantic pre-2000 Crayon flesh-colored lines—which may have made the burn worse. But it also may have eased the burn. There is no way of knowing anything for certain, other than right now I'm sufficiently high. Would I like to be higher? Absolutely. I am a lifelong drug addict. More is always the drug I prefer. If my eyes are still open enough that I'm able to glimpse more drugs, more money for drugs, or someone who may have one or both, then I want more. Always more of what makes me less.

My friend once composed a very beautiful suicide note while he was on a run he thought might end up in an overdose. He hit on a lot of points that resonated with me. A particular moment before puberty realizing, in a space that was completely neutral and devoid of sentimentality, that he'd never experience real happiness again. His was in a shopping mall. Anti-Satori or Satori. My moment like that came when I received the English award in the sixth grade. I accepted the trophy. People clapped. And I realized that *that* would be the apex of my life.

It wasn't very thrilling for an apex.

Something similar happened to me the first time I had sex. I was seventeen. Obviously, I'd obsessed over this moment. My girlfriend at the time just turned fifteen. She'd had a spider stick-and-poke tattooed on her right breast when she was twelve, but then she hit puberty and grew enormous tits, so by the time I got around to her, she had what looked like a thirty-year-old prison tattoo of an abstracted spider stretched across her outlandish right breast. We'd done the other stuff. I got my first blowjob at three in the afternoon on the sidewalk outside of a Burger King. I liked having my cock in a wet organ. So I'd assumed that sex would be an amplified version of that.

We were in my sister's room. It was 1991. She was a virgin (in hindsight, unlikely) and we fucked. I used a condom she stole from where she babysat—an ultra-thin Japanese number—and it broke. It didn't take long, I came too quickly, all what you'd expect. Then her pussy started dripping and we realized what had happened. I was momentarily worried I might have knocked her up, but then that feeling was instantly replaced by the awareness that I felt no differently now that I wasn't a virgin.

I'd thought, mistakenly, that perhaps sex would be the thing. By the thing, I mean multiform ideas and projections, primarily happiness, satisfaction, the absence of the gaping hole. The thing is many things. I walked home with my deliquescing cock in my work pants, pretty much having forgotten I may have impregnated a very young girl, wondering what the fuck it was going to take to make me feel whole again, now that I knew it wasn't sex.

Enter drugs.

2.

Sex works for a minute. Drugs work for a few. And when the mechanics of your dick get fucked up by your drugs, then your sexual interests become more mental than physical. In this way, you can make sex last longer, because you can sexualize everything. Say for example you're a sadist and you occasionally enjoy tying up your fake daughter with a Hitachi Magic Wand taped to her pussy for three hours on your bare mattress with her panties stuffed in her mouth and then taped shut so she can't make a sound, completely immobilized and trembling with agony and forced orgasms while you go shopping for groceries, stop to talk to a friend, and take some photographs of dying flowers in the sad autumnal afternoon. Boom, suddenly your sexual experience has lasted most of an afternoon. And that can sustain you a bit longer than in out in out, orgasm—momentary reprieve, then the monster reappears.

Drugs go in these places: the punctured vein, the nose, the asshole, the mouth. It's certainly no mistake that we use our holes to feed the hole. And I fill other people's holes with my dick when I can't find the drugs to fill the holes that feed my hole. When I have an orgasm I feel okay for a moment, then I feel like I need more, unless I'm sufficiently tired. When I get high myriad things occupy me, even if the drugs don't get me high enough. I'm itchy, I feel nauseous, I stare at a section of my wall for an hour, I nod off. I eat food off my sweater. I pick at myself. I take sips of water then let it fall out of my mouth onto my shirt. The after-effects of drugs are more consuming and satisfying than the after-effects of sex, which mostly just consist of some sweating, a rapid heartbeat, remote sleepiness and the odious task of affectionately interacting with whomever you just fucked.
Sex requires someone else, usually. Drugs are for being alone.

People who like to get fucked up with other people are not people I like to get fucked up with. Because getting fucked up is for doing alone. Or, very rarely, with someone who is likeminded and handles their drugs well; who doesn't talk too much and will let you rest your legs on their lap while you both silently take in the miraculous invention of the ceiling fan. With sex maybe you go buy a condom if someone's inclined, brush your teeth. With drugs you get dressed, you travel to sketchy areas of town, you anticipate the robbery that might happen; you get to talk to interesting characters, you get to engage in very subtle spy-like eye contact. You walk into various bathrooms of variously seedy bars. You enter hotel rooms and apartments that offer an endless variety of interior decor. There could be a fat, pasty schoolteacher, naked save dirty old Reeboks, looking dead on the couch; or an ornately scabrous guy, fetal, weeping in the corner, being used as an ashtray. Someone deep in debt could be tied to a desk chair being bothered. There may, on occasion, be a gloriously exotic woman with pendulous breasts swaying to no music in an open kimono in the centre of the room, a cigarette dangling from her lips, her eyes cast toward the heavens. She may be singing in Spanish. She may offer you a blowjob. She may be related to you. She may be your sister who you haven't seen in years. You may be attacked or hit with a stick, a bat, a bottle, a pipe, a wrench, a bike lock, the butt of a gun. You might hear a joke you've never heard before. You might learn that some junkies on couches are ex-physicists, and if you get high with the right person you may learn about string theory. You may get amazing dope, stepped on dope, burn bags, shit, garbage, uncut ambrosia, baby laxative, or told to get the fuck out. An intensely unpredictable and colorful world of threats, sex, product, ornament and conversation is made available to you the minute you step out of your home in pursuit of dope. Each time is like beginning a novel that may end either in death or enlightenment. There is the beauty of the greasy money, the transaction. The being sussed for a cop;

the display of your arms to prove you're not one. Personally, I don't like to do my drugs where I buy my drugs, so then there is the wonderful and difficult trip back home, knowing what you have in your pocket, wondering if it's good or not. You finger the drugs in your pocket nonstop. The subway always seems to be going too slow. You start to see cops everywhere. You get to experience the thrill of groundless paranoia. Once that's over, you're home. You clear the table off. You take the drugs out. You look at what you've got. You feel happy and excited. You set the stage, as it were. You bring out the implements, whatever your predilection may be. The cards, the razors, the water, the spoon, the knives, the needles, the papers—the dollar dollar bills. You create the perfect environment. You curate your high. You remove all extraneous stimuli from your surroundings. You adjust the lighting. You put on the appropriate clothes to match your particular drug (in my case a loose t-shirt, loose sweatshirt, loose sweatpants). You wash your face. You try to wait. And then when everything aligns, in the argot of my people, you *get it in you.*

After that, there is the high, if it works, and the previously mentioned array of phenomenon the drugs create: itchiness, vomiting, self-hypnosis, rapid cycling, elimination of thought, elimination of the muscles in the neck, back and face. And this is the experience, and this is a day's work, and this is your job, your real full-time job.

So I've most often chosen drugs for these reasons. Drugs take more time. And ultimately what I want is more and more of my time taken away from me, because when my time belongs to me, my time belongs to thinking. To me, there's nothing more intolerable than thinking. And whenever I find myself doing it, it's always about sex and drugs.

3.

Two things allowed me to make more and more work related to sex: when my ex-wife ex-wifed me and when I got over the fact of my mother. When I accepted that my mother had sucked dicks, been fucked and fucked others, lolled around naked, displayed her lithe body to eager suitors. She wasn't just my mother. It was an awful thing I'd done, defining her only as she related to me. But once I was free of that mentally, and once my ex-wife was no longer an audience I had to consider, I was free to make more work about sex.

I am terrified my mother will read this.

I had always *wanted* to make more work about sex. But I self-censored, I edited, I made sexual work obliquely. I never was straight forward about it. Which was unfair to me and also to the sketchy number of people who enjoy what I do.

My whole life I've been sexually obsessive. The first things I ever cut up and put on my wall as a child were bra and panty ads from my mother's Eaton's catalogue. This was when my age was in the single digits. My father was very open about sex. By that I mean I saw his pornography, and I saw him fuck women who weren't my mother. He also talked about it endlessly in detail, sometimes using me as a ploy to get laid.

I also used to read my parents newspaper on the weekends. The images that caught my interest the most—this was in the late seventies and early eighties, when there were good solid news pictures out there—were at the back of the Toronto Sun. They were ads for X-rated movies. I clipped those out too. All of this before my dick had ever functioned as anything but a way to eliminate urine from my bladder. Years and years before my first erection.

I looked at my father's porn magazines at this age too. I was less interested in the tits, asses and pussies displayed in overly lit spreads, and more interested in the back of the magazines, where there were ads for other magazines—fetish magazines. I was drawn to black-and-white pictures of women tied up. Of women with gags in their mouths and blindfolds over their eyes. The darker and stranger the imagery was, the more I felt drawn to it. Women in cages, women on leashes. And the most compelling feature I was interested in, that remains with me now, was on the face of some random unknown woman, *an appearance of being overwhelmed.* I was ten when I first realized I liked this.

They say that fetishes are the product of moments from childhood, but my attraction to this imagery predated any trauma or explanatory instance. I imagine it's a result of my fetishizing these images as a child, that now in my life, I photograph, archive and document almost all of my sexual activity. I don't really look at it, but I get satisfaction out of knowing I have three hard drives full of videos and pictures of innumerable women in varying states of pleasure, distress, confinement, pain, enjoyment and frustration.

I think, through sentimentally enduring the prosaic slop of Milan Kundera in my early twenties, I read a quote from Goethe which I can only paraphrase badly, which was itself paraphrased, that went something like, "Men use sex as a way to capture images of women, to keep as Polaroids in their mind, to be looked at and consumed in their old age when they can no longer be sexual." Obviously, Polaroid and Goethe in the same sentence means I've greatly confused the sentence I'm recalling. But I've come to see the truth in this. Especially now as I'm getting older and my own sex equipment is less reliable than it once was. I will one day be able to live out my entire sexual life by browsing videos and photographs I've taken.

Sometimes when I was collecting obscure fetish magazines, I'd see a very attractive woman, photographed in say 1973, and I'd think about how if she were still alive, she'd be some old woman somewhere, with a life, problems, medical issues, trouble and happiness. Maybe she'd done it for money once. Maybe she'd loved it. Maybe she'd forgotten. But I've always found it both sad and interesting to think of these women, frozen pornographically in time, out in the world, waiting their turn at the oncologist's office, or cold and ashen underground.

How quickly points get lost in the glossolalia of one's own self-absorption.

If I can put together the fragments of an idea from two days ago through a fog of no sleep and more dope, this is what I am trying to say. If you make work about sex, you don't need to leave the house for anything more than drugs, food, smokes and liquids. The women and girls will start coming to you. They will come to you through the internet, emails, friends of friends. They will come to you like rats onto the streets from flooding sewers. I stay in my dank work suite and pump out writing and art about sex, and it develops a life of its own in the public without my having to go anywhere. Then the greasy tendrils span out and curl back into my home various girls and women who want certain things.

I'm not interested in the ones who are drawn to the creator of the work, I'm interested in the ones who are drawn to the content. Star fuckers have yappy mouths and lay flat on the bed with their eyes wide in awe. Little perverts enraptured by content lay as they are told to lay, and I can make their eyes do countless things.

That has been the benefit of being divorced and getting over my mom's sex life.

4.

The things I've done for sex and drugs: unspeakable. The things sex and drugs have done for me: my entire output. And enough material to last me another lifetime as an artist.

It's terroristic outside today. Someone or multiple people are shooting guns in the Parliament. My mother wrote me that she "hoped I was" watching the news. Why this was her hope for me, I cannot say. I was not watching. I watched briefly, I got the gist, then I left in pursuit of more dope. What I love about drug addicts, one of many things, is that they don't care about the news. News is an abstraction. The only news is who's holding, who's got good dope, bad dope, where's the cops. That's it. So when I step into Alfie's this afternoon to score off Bobby, the same bar I used to go buy dope in twenty years ago, even though the live news is playing on a shitty stolen flat screen television, no one is really aware of what it means. Addicts stop growing and paying attention to the trembling world out there the minute their addiction gets its hooks in them. That's why junkies and prostitutes often look like actors from another time. The minute you get into your dope is the minute you stop progressing in the progressive world. No need for new clothes, new music, new hair styles. Drugs are beautiful in the way they create a singularly focused mind.

Personally, I've never felt safer than when I'm in a dark room full of dealers, pimps, hookers and addicts. I feel so much safer in those places than I do when I step out of them. I understand the movements, the sounds and smells and manners of that environment. Out in the other world, cars honk and I twitch. I can't tell who is a threat and who isn't. I don't understand who people are. Inside of my drugs and the places my drugs live I feel like a rattlesnake in the desert. I move like water down rivulets and settle into pockets for blind days on end. I feel safe in the places most fear. I feel fear in the places most feel are safe.

But it's terroristic outside today. I saw green jeeps and docile Canadian machine guns. A Persian man near skid row said, "Give me a hug," and it looked like he might have been wearing a suicide vest. It was the most tempting hug I've been offered all year.

This is inside information. This is how it really is if you're an addict, the real type, the authentic lover of narcotics. The first time you decide to pick up, you're doing drugs. After that though, drugs are doing you. You're what's in drug's veins. You're feeding drugs. Your money and your soul are getting shot into drug's system and making drugs stronger and stronger. Drugs have a problem with me. Drugs need me. I course through drugs veins like a viscous blue bolt of depleting energy and sad aging desperation. I make drugs smile.

5.

My most recent ex-girlfriend was the most complementary any person had ever been to me in my life until we broke up. She said she liked how eccentric I was. She liked that I eat at the same pho restaurant every day. She liked that the manager would sit at my table and we'd talk about seventies politics. She liked the strange people who were drawn to me. She liked my clockless lifestyle. She truly admired my eccentricity, and she was very generous and warm and loving. But I think ultimately I was just too much for her, and I kept so much to myself.

The woman before her thought my ostensible eccentricity was an act. She told me I *chose* to be unemployable. She'd spent too much time around people in the The Program if she honestly believed that shit.

The girl before her told me she watched us fucking from seven feet above us. She claimed to have watched us from the corner of the ceiling. She said she liked seeing how her body fucked mine while she hovered above us. She'd be frozen for a half hour, waxy, a glass of water in her hand, cigarette burnt to nothing in her mouth, eyes fixed on some phantom on a drab patch of ceiling. Schizophrenia is a kind of eccentricity.

My second ex-wife liked the *style* of my eccentricity. She liked how we appeared to be a very eccentric couple. She wanted Grey Gardens on the outside, Martha Stewart on the inside. She was all about appearances. Which made sense as she was beautiful but fundamentally lacking in depth.

If you don't know that someone is a drug addict, a pervert, a photography addict, scraping by on zero money and habituated into certain habits as the result of PTSD, you may mistake them for an eccentric. But I don't have a superfluous cane or a transatlantic accent. I'm just a collection of appearances all designed to mask and keep cozy an array of symptoms, traumas, predilections and unrelenting vengefulness.

6.

Today might have been the closest I've come to being murdered. I was shocked at my complete lack of shock. I wasn't interested at all in the fact that I may have been subjected to a gruesome and frightful death with a heavy, violently grey bike lock. That I managed to talk my way out of being murdered is both a testament to my charisma and to my putting dope before my own life. I talked my way out of the situation not because I was worried I might die, but because I was worried this guy might fuck up my ability to score on that block. If he murdered me, I would not only be unable to get high that afternoon, I'd be unable to get high ever again.

I was photographing a basketball net from far away with the zoom on my camera. This was stupid. So, of course this guy ramps up on me sketched out thinking I'm trying to take his picture (which, I wanted to say, what are you a fucking celebrity? You're a dope slanging parolee on a girl's mountain bike. *I did not say this*). Many times I was called a goof and many curses were put upon my mother, particularly on her vagina and what it may have to endure. Having spent time in rehab I know that goof is death language, and if I were a jailbird I would have had no choice but to fight him to the death. Once he called me goof and saw that I didn't go for his throat he realized I wasn't a threat, so I was lambasted with a sequence of goofs, fuck your mothers, white snakes and the like. He picked up his bicycle with shocking grace and brought it from far above his head to within an inch of my face and then stopped. He took the bike lock off and began swinging it. He would not shut up. I noticed as I spoke to him that my heart rate was not changing. I was not sweating. I felt neither weak nor adrenalized. No dry mouth, stutter, bowel or urinary looseness. I quietly kept telling him that no, I was not taking his picture. I attempted to point out to him the photographic opportunity offered to me by the startling contrast of a basketball net being used by people in shorts fore-grounded by piles of snow from the indoor ice rink. I knew he wasn't listening, because he wouldn't stop talking. What he said was you're going to die, goof, your mother's pussy, white snake, rat, goof, gonna fucking kill you, you take my picture, snake, you're gonna fucking die, see this lock, motherfucker and goof. But I've learned one thing over the years that more successful animal species know intuitively: do not show fear. The fact that I *felt* no fear was making it much easier. And while he was slic-ing his Kryptonite lock through the air mere centimeters from my frangible skull, while people stopped and stared, while he screamed the same sequence of non-word signal epithets over and over, I just began to walk away, arms gesturing as if to say yeah, I know it's a dumb move with the camera, but no, I was not taking your picture. Occasionally I'd point to the basketball net. I did not speed up or slow down. I did not once look back. The sound of the lock splitting the air became more distant, the cries of goof and snake harder to hear, and eventually I realized I was fine.

If you don't think drugs are fun you're not doing them right. If you do think drugs are fun you're not doing them right. Booze though, that's where the trouble lies, and I haven't touched it in years.

7.

I showed what I'd written so far here to someone I love because this woman wants to know "all about me." She said she liked it. She is my sister. Our relationship precludes her having any moral issues with pretty much anything I think. She said that she thought it may be better if I focused more on the sex addiction aspect, because sex addiction isn't written about much. She said that a great deal had already been written about artists and their drugs and alcohol.

The reason I want to write about drugs is that I don't believe anyone has done a proper job of it. That it has been tried over and over and that there is already so much writing devoted to the topic doesn't deter me. I also think I'm willing to be more honest than most other writers have been, and not ornament the language with psychedelic verbs or glamorizing adjectives. It's not free association. It's not prosaic. It's not about the great and holy union between drugs and art. I'm writing about being a common drug addict. That I make art is irrelevant. No matter what my job were, I would still be a drug addict.

Writing about sex addiction has the unfortunate side effect, I imagine, of decreasing the sympathy of the reader. I need the sympathy. How could I be cared for as a narrator, if I confess to the fact that I would fuck probably seventy to eighty percent of all living women? If I told you that I sometimes catch myself looking at and wanting to fuck teenagers? If I said that, as a forty-year-old man, I've spent the last month fucking a twenty-year-old, often in very antisocial ways, and my only regret about the entire relationship between us is that I met her a month after she stopped being nineteen? Some fringe social scientist has recently coined the term Ephebophila to describe this desire. It's a neologism created by a late phase pedophile to justify and medicalize his interest in non-quite-adult girls. The putative ephebophiliac is sexually drawn to girls and boys between the ages of fourteen and nineteen. That is to say, in the midst of and immediately after the shock of puberty; right before gravity, stress and the environment begin to weather and humanize the body. By humanize, I mean make more human through the patina of suffering. This is the age where bodies are perfect, fecund, shiny sex machines. Biology and prehistoric imperatives have designated this age as the most sexually appealing. I could employ the excuse that it's not my fault it's only been a few millennia since my ancestors were walking on all fours, that a part of my brain is still hardwired to find teenagers attractive. Even considering it's an impulse I can easily dismiss, who will want to hear about it, never mind sympathize with this predilection? But sure, I'm a sex addict. I go to meetings. I am powerless over sex. I've fucked unfuckable things. I've done awful deeds. I've put my dick where I wouldn't put my best shoes. That it's not been written about enough, that drugs have been written about too much, isn't enough reason for me to alter—through pressure, shame, or a desire for originality—what I'm writing right now.

In any case, opiates. Chemical castration doesn't work, because the dick of the addict lives in his mind. To make your sex organs forever limpid and unusable only leads to more rage. Opiates however, are, more than therapy has ever been—more than chemical castration could ever be—the most effective way to manage my sex addiction. A commitment to opioids renders your dick a small sad tube for waste elimination. It's hard to get it up and you can rarely have an orgasm. And if you can get it up, it's not on your mind anyway. Opiates erase sex from the menu.

Knowing women who have dated junkies, it's a strange point of pride that I have never spat on a girl's back to fake orgasm. I just claim exhaustion and a congenital difficulty with orgasming.

So, I can with confidence posit that my drug addiction has been the greatest remedy for my sex addiction. I still look at women and girls all the time, but now they're ornamental. I've returned to beauty, and left carnality somewhere in the empty dime bag.

Anyway, there's some writing on sex addiction for you, darling sister.

8.

Right now I'm worried I could be in over my head. I'm very weak. I've spent all day in bed. When I've tried to go out and smoke, it's been hard to get my coat on, and I've only been able to smoke half the cigarette before I need to come back in and lie down. William Eggleston once said that his entire body of work was an attempt to write a novel. I think my entire body of work is a suicide note. But considering how I feel at this exact moment, this might be the most urgent and genuine version of that expression thus far. I feel nervous and rattled, and I'm not sure if powdering 2mg of Clonazepam and putting it up my nose will calm me down, or increase the weakness I'm feeling.

Schopenhauer said that love, sex, physical attraction, desires for certain body types, big hips, tall men—all of it was a prehistoric propulsion towards procreation. I think that sounds right.

Bobby Fischer was a notorious recluse and horrible anti-Semite who let chess crack his brain, or who excelled at chess because his brain was cracked. His dying words were, "Nothing soothes pain like the human touch." I also think that's right.

Albert Ayler tried and tried to get clean but ended up walking into the ocean. I think he made the best music of the 20th century.

I'm not used to being touched. My particular sexual behavior precludes allowing myself to be handled softly or lovingly. It breaks the fourth wall. But I could use it now. This doesn't make a whole lot of sense, but I feel like I need to write these things down because I'm not sure how much longer I'll be able to. I love my sister, I love one of my ex-girlfriends, I love my two best friends, I love my mother.

*

In the end, I only believe in Siddhartha Gautama and Bertrand Russell. And although I've published many things indicating otherwise, I believe the only truly original artists of the last one hundred odd years are Vladimir Nabokov and Patricia Highsmith.

9.

False alarm. Woke up eleven hours after I wrote the previous passage with a shriveled chunk of pear on my sweatshirt and a lava flow of dried blood that had oozed out of my nose, settled in my moustache and plastered itself to my top lip.

> *"Many addicts were not held enough as infants, were not soothed enough or were left alone or with strangers. These things are traumatic to the developing child. As children many addicts experienced abandonment, were sent away, or were devalued or rejected by their caregivers in some way. All of these things constitute abuse and lead to problems later on."*

I was told my mother had postpartum depression. I know my father did. I don't remember being touched much. Psychiatrists talk a lot about self-soothing, which can extend from touching yourself lightly with your fingertips to putting a needle in your arm, to pacing, to preparing one's suicide like a recipe for risotto.

Irony: Hydromorph Contin beads are very strong and almost impossible to break down into powder. It takes a ridiculous amount of muscle strength to grind the beads into something you can inject or plug or insufflate. That junkies don't have much strength in their arms makes this type of opiate horribly challenging, although the payoff is enormous.

Comedy: Most "harm reduction" or opiate user websites talk about how hard it is to break Hydromorph Contin down into a powder because junkies don't have the muscle strength to grind the beads into a form you can inject or plug or insufflate.

So, it's not all melancholy, sweating and unrelenting itchiness. Occasionally one of the doses you stumble on is comedy.

10.

Important to remember this is all fiction. Directed to myself or to you—it doesn't matter. It's all fiction.

Remember though that all writing is fiction.

Woke up panicked today when I realized I'd be five days short of my prescribed Morphine, and it's fucking raining and snowing here and with only four hundred odd dollars in the bank I'd need at least three hundred to fill the gap I've made for myself to avoid being dopesick. So I did the usual, skipped lunch and prayed to God Bobby was at Alfie's.

My nose is fucking obliterated but I'm still committed to this vow of never injecting, because of my dad. Because of my dad injecting me; because of me tying my dad off and injecting him. I tell myself the minute I use needles is when I'm a real junkie. I know it's complete bullshit. I've been a real junkie for twenty-four years now. So today, since I can barely breathe through my nose, it's going to have to go up my ass.

The entire walk from the subway to the corner I prayed Bobby would be there. He wasn't, but I saw this dude Zeke who had once big upped my shoes inside Alfie's. Zeke saw me across the street and we did the nod or whatever, then I asked if Bobby was around. Zeke said he wasn't, but he asked what I wanted. I said down. He said yeah I got that. And so after a conversation of less than ten words I'm home with eight 200mg caps of Morphine. $400.00.

I needed to be responsible with the pills if I was going to make it to the day my prescription got refilled. But of course I wasn't. I put four-hundred milligrams up my ass and swallowed another two hundred. Now I'm properly high.

*

I'm forever aiming for high again; higher than I think is safe but not so high that I know I'll die.

Or that's what I tell myself. The truth is I probably flirt with death on a regular basis.

11.

I've already said an addict is a person with holes. Those holes are either congenital, shot out, or carved and eaten away at until what remains is this thing, the hole.

The hole can never be filled.

The thing most likely to fill the hole is love, but love is fleeting, unreliable, conditional. Drugs are unconditional. Certain ways of being sexual are unconditional. There's an old story about a boy trying to ward off a flood by sticking his thumb in a hole in the wall. I don't relate. The character I relate to most is Daffy Duck. Sometimes Daffy would get hit by buckshot. He'd put his finger in a hole in his cartoon body, and then another hole would start squirting liquid. He'd be busy with all his fingers and toes trying to plug the holes that leaked, but the holes were always more numerous than his digits, than his methods for filling them. I am Daffy Duck. I cannot fill my holes. The best I've come up with is something like a spiritual tampon that absorbs the hurt and keeps things blocked up for a bit, but the toxic pus of the hole always needs out, or ectopic shock sets in. I've felt the masculine equivalent of that shock. I've left a certain hole plugged a certain way for too long and it's backfired. I've had seizures, divorces, overdoses, fugue states, failed suicide attempts, fits of anger and dark sexual misadventures. I'm forty years old as I write this. And what I've learned, if I've learned anything at all, is that you need to reconcile living with your insatiable hole. You don't have to love it, but you need to accept it. I've come to accept that I'm a fundamentally incomplete creature. Parts of me are missing. I can't reassemble myself, as much as I've tried.

12.

Three days straight I've woken up at 2:24 in the morning, which is around the time I imagine my sister is washing her perfect body and getting ready to go to school, to do her MFA across the pond. I don't believe in numbers. I only believe in the following, in no order of significance: drugs, art, sex, non-duality. The self is a giant problem. The idea that we even have one is a delusion. I remember in the movie Back to The Future, Michael J. Fox is battling to keep a Polaroid of his family from slowly erasing into a white square of nothingness. Most of my adult life has been trying to find a way to laboriously erase the same Polaroid. The Polaroid isn't of my family, or even of me, but a representation of an idea I have—of something called my Self.

I've lost fifteen pounds this month. Not intentionally, but as the result of chronic pain eliminating my appetite, and maybe because of drugs, if in fact I'm doing them. This is erasure. I remember once seeing my psychiatric records, and my doctor referring to my "anorexia." I didn't realize until then that anorexia isn't just an eating disorder. Literally, it's just not taking in enough food to keep yourself at a healthy weight. I am anorexic then, but not because of any concerns about body image. I am anorexic in that, if only subconsciously, I am trying to erase myself. Each time I make a painting, I give away part of myself. I give it to the world. The world isn't asking, but I give. Each of these sentences are pieces of myself I am shedding off and hoping won't rebound and stick to me. Each time I do drugs—if I do them at all—I am trying to slow down my mind to the point of stopping my mind to the point of no mind at all. Bumper sticker says: Know Jesus, Know Peace / No Jesus, No Peace. But there is also: No Mind, No Death. If I can take the slimy orb my skull encases and whittle away at it, through putting art or ideas out into the world, then I can extricate myself of this thing my mind mistakenly calls Mind. I can come closer to Death, and No Death. I can live forever in not living.

Not living is another way to exist in the world.

When I have sex, I give myself away to whoever I'm fucking. Some part of me leaves when they do. I don't do very much, but what I do I do wholeheartedly, all of it with complete *self-abandon*. I am trying to abandon an illusory self. It's like when my father left and I never heard from him again. He left me, but he also disavowed me. If all things I manifest through my mind are my children, I want to abandon every last one of them. My inner child is not something I want to nurture and care for, it is something I want to leave in a basket on the steps of a convent.

I have made myself look very bad. I have written down the worst of me. I feel an echo of shame but mostly a sense of self-loathing. Shame is a feeling people with beliefs tend to experience. Not having any real beliefs of my own, I tend towards clinical self-hatred.

All my work is a suicide note then. This is a suicide note. This is work. I feel that I'm never not working. And the work I'm never not doing is the work of undoing myself. I didn't ask to be here, and I'm hoping I can, in ways where nobody is aware of it—because it seems like I'm contributing, be it through art or orgasms or essays—slowly walk away from this place, this 'self' I had no choice but to inhabit. And for a moment, a very brief one, a small number of people might ask "Where'd Brad go?" But then as now, they'll go back to their drinks, they'll go back to gossiping, making plans, talking about their shoes and their symposiums, and I'll be an ephemeral shape losing focus down an alley, scattering behind me paintings and writing and women's underwear as I go.

The world will go on. It went on before I was here, it goes on now while I'm barely here, and it will go on soon when I'm gone. I had a nice time. And I had the worst time.

And I love every single creature on this planet.

UNEXPURGATED CRAIGSLIST AD

The following is an unedited craigslist ad I attempted to post in 2015. It was rejected, as in my fervor to provide immense detail, I violated, stupidly and disrespectfully in hindsight, the privacy of the woman the ad was intended to reach. I learned from this experience, with the help of Dr. Leslie Morris, to not post anything on the internet while in the throes of a manic episode ever again.

L OOKING FOR HANNAH ALCORN OR ANYONE WHO MAY
know her whereabouts. Last known to be living in Ade-
laide, Australia, possibly under a different name. Black hair,
blue eyes, petite figure; mostly wears black, prone to leather. This
describes her sixteen years ago. She'll be fifty-six years old now,
her appearance will have changed. Originally from Glasgow;
speaks with a thick, working-class Glaswegian accent. Feisty, per-
verted, well-acquainted with a vast number of profanities and
inclined to use them. This is not a 'missed connection.' I am
attempting to find Hannah, as she seems to have disappeared
about nine years ago. I just want to know that she's alive and well.

Maybe it'd be best to write this ad directly to Hannah. She'd recognize my writing and the stories from when we knew each other.
But if you do know Hannah Alcorn, or know someone who may,
please get in touch. I'm only seeking assurance that she's okay.
My name is Brad Phillips. Tell anyone who might know. Write
my message in your Australian sky and invoice me via PayPal.

Dear Hannah,

We first 'met' in a Yahoo trivia chat room in the spring of 2001.
I wish I could remember your handle because it was good. I
have no idea what mine was, but it might have been Oprah,
because that was the handle I used to play Scrabble at isc.ro and

other places online at the time. At first, we didn't speak to each other. You'd just type 'lol' at me whenever I brutally insulted the people I was beating. I used to be an abrasive asshole on the internet back then. You weren't very good at trivia, but that wasn't something I gave a shit about. Too much time spent in bars and in books, an ability to type ridiculously fast, that's why I dominated that trivia chat room. I enjoyed trash-talking much more than I enjoyed playing trivia. Then one day you popped up on the sidebar. [Blank] was inviting me to a private chat, did I want to accept?

I have always accepted the conversation of strange women, and it was no different then. My girlfriend was teaching or in class more than twelve hours a day, and I'd recently started making enough money from art that I didn't need a job, so all I really did was sit at home, getting high and masturbating. I also played trivia with strangers, and unleashed my intense anger about the life I'd gotten myself stuck in onto undeserving, probably very nice trivia players online. As soon as we started to chat privately there, I never played another game of trivia.

You asked me first for a photo, and gave me your email address. The internet was an adolescent still; I couldn't just attach one in the chat room. I sent you a photo of myself with a well-deserved black eye, a shaved head and a new beard grown to cover a scar on my cheek created by twelve stitches, scar and source injury also well-deserved. People did this back then, pic for pic. I'd honestly never done it before. You sent me back a photo of yourself and that's when I knew I was in trouble. You had the blackest natural hair I'd ever seen, your bangs cut straight above your dramatic eyebrows, the rest ending just around your chin. All of it framing the most shocking blue eyes. You bore an uncanny resemblance to Marina Oswald (née Prusakova) at the time of her marriage to Lee Harvey Oswald. I was obsessed with Marina then, having been deep into books about JFK's assassination and all the attendant conspiracies.

We then began doing what I now know to be common: we talked constantly and told each other everything about our lives. I was miserable, twenty-seven years old, and about to marry my partner who I'd been with since I was twenty-four. I wanted out desperately and had for years, but for some reason the best idea I could come up with to achieve this goal was to ask her to marry me.

For you it was much worse, though we were both stuck in situations we hadn't anticipated. You were living in Australia with an abusive asshole who didn't reveal his abusive tendencies until you'd agreed to move there to be near his parents. You had two small children with him. You had no legal status there and leaving Paul would mean losing custody of your kids, something you just couldn't allow.

The time difference made it perfect for us to talk. You were on the other side of the world. I'd wake up in the morning and lay in bed until I heard my soon-to-be-wife Anna leave for school, then I'd join the Yahoo chatroom just after you put your kids to bed. Paul would usually be out getting drunk. We'd talk about the seemingly universal disdain for Australians—their accents, their strange lack of cultural contributions, their Neanderthal version of rugby. Sometimes Paul would come home and flop his fat drunk ass down on the couch behind you and start snoring, oblivious to his undersexed and ultra-compelling wife sitting on her computer. We'd often chat while he snored behind you.

You thought you were too old for me. I was twenty-seven; you were forty. I told you that you weren't too old for me, and you weren't. I think it took you awhile to believe that I meant it.

I still hadn't heard you speak, and I wanted to. I didn't want the lag of the internet, the ttyl's and brb's, but you were shy about your accent. Later, I'd love the filthy things you'd say in that accent. I never told you, but I only understood about ninety percent of what you said to me. What I missed I got to make up, and it added to my picture of you—talking to me in your bathroom, your kids asleep in the next room, your husband and his parents all around you. You'd whisper "Bradley" and tell me what you were doing with the small frozen dildo you pulled out of its hiding place in the freezer, trying to talk to me while you felt how cold it was inside your ass. I'd never and still haven't met another woman who required ice cold implements inside her body to get off. It was charming.

You were a teacher, and you told me you'd get turned on by the sweaty seventeen-year-old football players in your class, and at lunch or on breaks you'd go into the bathroom, squat on the toilet lid facing the wall and rub your clit against the cold steel fixtures of the toilet.

Even now, sexual memories of you can sidetrack me.

The first conversation we had on the phone, you told me about your parents. Your father volunteered to fight in Vietnam, even though he was older than the kids being sent to slaughter from America. You told me he was feared in the part of Glasgow you grew up in; his face was expressionless, or rather always locked in some menacing non-expression. But the face people most associated with him was the "Glasgow Smile." He only gave it, never wore it himself. He'd fought in Korea, for the South Africans in Angola during the CIA proxy war with Cuba. He trained Uruguayan paramilitary officers in advanced interrogation techniques while you wished to be a princess—a Scotch one. He was a mercenary, upset he'd missed the Second World War. You told me about being a kid, nine or ten years old, sitting on his lap, asking him how many people he'd killed. He told you he knew the number but that numbers couldn't answer the question. That one life was worth more numbers than others. Someone could count for three, even ten, while someone else didn't count at all. He told you, tiny Hannah, that he was a balloon full of death, and that each time he killed someone he felt their life-force fill his body. He said he felt gigantic, stuffed to bursting with the souls of innumerable dead.

So, you peed yourself in his lap. I would have too. Then he threw you across the room, gifting you that small scar under your eye which you would always apologize self-consciously for. I thought it looked beautiful.

Your mother was in an asylum in Glasgow.

Time on the internet since I met you has taught me that it wasn't unique our correspondence became so sexual so fast. Once you got over your shyness about your accent—although the shyness never completely vanished, making you speak in an endearing whisper much of the time—we began talking on the phone a lot more. The chat room and our time there became the first memory we shared, the first historical remnant of our 'affair,' which was the word I used to describe what we were having in my head. I was young, and back then the idea of an affair seemed glamorous. It seemed like something people much older than me did; something people your age did. We spoke every single day. If for some reason we couldn't, we emailed each other. I changed my password multiple times a week. I was paranoid of Anna finding out, which was stupid, as it would have been an ideal way to end the relationship.

The wedding was approaching. You never discouraged me. One would think that getting to know you would have given me the courage to call it off, but it never crossed my mind. I only became more paranoid that Anna might find out about you. One day I heard her opening our apartment door while I was jerking off, close to having an orgasm with you on the phone. It was then I decided my home was no longer safe for us. So began the complex labyrinth of payphones and lies about why I was leaving the house.

You emailed me pornographic photos of yourself, and I'd send you my own versions in kind. I shared my computer with Anna, so I never downloaded the photos, but I printed them and hid them in an envelope deep in a box full of papers.

My friend at the time was making underwear out of vintage rock t-shirts. Boy's y-front briefs. I showed you photos and you liked them, so I bought you a pair—a size small made from a Journey tour shirt. I sent them to you in the mail, along with a handwritten letter, and you sent me photos of yourself wearing them. You were the first woman I knew who was good at photographing herself sexually. I asked you to wear the underwear for four days in a row and send it back to me. I realized you couldn't send it to mine and Anna's apartment, so I gave you my mother's address. This became the love nest of our affair, an element I found alluring because it reminded me of movies.

When my mother called and said there was a package for me, I picked a fight with Anna and told her I needed space. Then, after watching Jeopardy with my mom, I went upstairs and opened the envelope. The underwear was wrapped in plastic, something you did so that they would still smell fresh, and I manipulated them until the white-streaked strip of crotch fabric was visible, which I then buried my nose in. You smelled so very good. Without thinking, I licked the crusted stains that your body produced, then began to masturbate. I put my cock in your panties and came all over the crotch, adding my DNA to yours.

That night, I called you from my mother's house and told you what I'd done. You asked me to mail them back to you so you could wear them unwashed. I thought, 'I love this woman.' You promised you'd mail me more.

A few days later Anna and I were married.

After the wedding, something strange and beautiful happened.

Anna seemed bored of me. I should acknowledge that I am stupid, often arrogant and unthinking, and that at this time in my life I was not a good or caring person. Coming to know you may have been what turned the light of relative goodness on in me. Still, I was behaving in a morally reprehensible fashion. I remember noticing I felt no guilt whatsoever. At times, I suspected Anna's putative boredom was an act, a sign she knew my mind was occupied by someone else. Maybe she thought her cold shoulder would sweat it out of me. I would not sweat. I found it hard to believe she might be onto me, as I'd kept secrets with the skill and fortitude of a CIA bureau chief my entire life, but nevertheless, I presumed I was under suspicion, and ramped up the secrecy.

I started calling you from different places. I would call you from the bank of payphones at the Sheraton Hotel at Queen and Bay Street. I would call you from the payphones at the St. Clair Center underground mall, next to the Druxy's, which emitted such a strong scent of pastrami that I'd always get a sandwich after. I would call you from the payphones at Mount Sinai Hospital, typically after Anna had gone to bed; the people on the phones around me were often weeping about sick and dying loved ones while you described to me in real time the ways in which you were masturbating. I would call you from the single payphone at the corner of King Street and Spadina Avenue, which was hidden inside of a pay parking lot and obscured by a bush. This allowed me to masturbate freely without fear of being caught. I would call you from the payphones at York University, near Benton Library, where I'd sometimes meet Anna after school to go grocery shopping. I got a bicycle and told Anna my doctor had suggested exercise for my depression. It was true that he'd suggested this, but I only ever used the bicycle to get from our apartment to a payphone.

I also had a second secret at that time: my drug habit. My neighbor four doors down let me store my dope in his mailbox for seventy-five dollars a month. Each night I'd tell Anna I needed to go for a ride, then I'd stop to 'check the mail' and ride to whichever phone booth I wanted to call you from.

At eight in the evening here it would be eight-thirty in the morning there. You didn't start work at school until ten, which gave us a good amount of time to talk. I was moved by your devotion, working so hard to get your kids fed and off to school so you could spend your remaining minutes with me until you had to leave. You'd change clothes on the phone, telling me what you were putting on (or taking off), eat breakfast on the phone, brush your teeth, pee. Sometimes you'd be late for work because it was so hard to hang up.

After we finally did, I would ride my bike to some grassy part of the city with my 'mail' burning a hole in my back pocket. I'd get high and lay in the grass, playing our conversation over in my head, imagining you next to me, your head on my shoulder. The smell of your hair was unknown to me, but I could conjure up whiffs of exotic shampoos. I was young then, and amazed that the sky I looked up at, smoggy and starless, was the same sky that warmed your body while you taught history to high schoolers.

If Anna were awake when I got home, my night would consist of tiresome bullshitting. If she was sleeping, I'd jerk off to photos of you. In the morning, once she left, I would eat breakfast quickly then head to a payphone. There, you'd tell me all about your day. You would be exhausted after work, after your kids' homework, after fighting with or being humiliated by Paul. You needed to masturbate to fall asleep, and I'd wait while you went to the freezer for your ice-cold dildo and butt plug. When you came back I would tell you all the things I was going to do to you, and you'd have three or four orgasms with your hand over your mouth. You were shy about the way you sounded when you came. Hearing you orgasm with your hand pressed against the phone like that, to muffle your voice, I could have sworn those were some of the most beautiful sounds the natural world ever produced.

Paul's parents cared for you more than they cared for their son. They knew he was a shiftless alcoholic and that you were the one raising their grandchildren. I was shocked when one day you told them about me. You told them there was a man far away who loved you, who didn't care that you had kids, who would be honored to help you raise them. I felt those things and told you that. It remains one of the more bizarre aspects of my past that I could call you when your husband was home and his parents would pick up, say hello to me, then pass to the phone to you.

I can't remember exactly how or when it happened, but at some point it became okay for me to call at any time. Even if Paul answered I'd ask for you. I think you told him you'd made a friend online. That he never got jealous seemed to prove just how much he took you for granted. Your children knew my name and you would have them say hi to me in their thick Scottish/Australian accents. I wanted desperately to rescue you, but I didn't have the money to bring you and your children to Canada.

My life had become a complicated spycraft web of calls and clockwatching which you were the center of. I barely painted. I had six pairs of your panties hidden in my safety deposit box. I imagined what it would be like to have two small children. I liked what I imagined.

In the middle of October 2001, Anna and I got into a fight. Having no place to escape to in the city, I went to my parents for a few days. There, I could call you as much as I wanted. Anna called me the second day I was there and said what she said in every fight we'd ever had, which was that "maybe we should just break up." Each time she said this in the past, no matter how much I was dying to end it, for reasons I didn't understand, I would convince her we could work things out. But that day I just said "Okay, let's break up." Anna was stunned. She cried for a minute and then another strange thing happened: she was fine. She agreed. It was *amicable.* My ego proven wrong again, it turned out her boredom hadn't just been a ruse to flush you out. She actually just didn't like me anymore. I was relieved that I managed to get out of my marriage without having to reveal what I'd been up to with you.

"Tell me what kind of pictures turn you on," you asked me one day. You preferred I masturbate to images of you instead of depressing pornography; not out of narcissism, but because you knew that watching pornography made me feel like shit. You were shocked and charmed by my answer: I wanted you to photograph yourself from a distance, sitting in office chairs while wearing formal clothing with your legs open just enough so I could see your panties, which I told you had to be white.

I think you must have used your best friend Nisha's office. Judging from your perfectly nasty office outfits, either the school you taught at was more formal than I'd realized, or you had clothing from past office work. You did such a good job for me. I have no idea why at the time that was what turned me on, but you nailed it with every photo. Photos from fifteen feet away, your legs crossed at the ankles, a small triangle of visible white cotton resting on the chair. Photographs of you from behind, picking a pencil up off the floor with your legs perfectly straight so that your skirt hiked up enough to show that same white fabric. You, sitting in an ergonomic chair, one finger in your lipsticked mouth, legs wipe open, staring into the camera. No one had ever been so thoughtful or had ever taken the time to indulge me the way you did.

Even though I hadn't met you, I was falling in love with you.

*

I didn't want to explain to my friends why my marriage had ended so soon after they'd taken the time to come to the wedding. I decided to move to Vancouver, which was either closer to you backwards, or even further way, I can't remember. Anna gave me the four thousand dollars we'd received at the wedding so I could travel and set myself up on the other side of the country. She was kind that way.

I stayed at my parents house and Anna stayed at our old apartment. We got together a week before I was to move to Vancouver, because Anna wanted to finish writing the thank you notes we needed to send to everybody who came to our wedding. It was awkward sitting on the couch with her, all my things gone, signing those cards. Anna noticed I'd gotten much thinner and became upset, assuming I'd lost weight because I was depressed. The truth was I'd lost so much weight because I could do dope more freely now without her and I wasn't expected to eat at certain times of the day. I let her be sad and I comforted her, enjoying the sympathy and affection it elicited. Then she said, "We should probably have sex one last time, shouldn't we?"

Sex had felt wrong for a while. I didn't like that I was imagining you while I was inside of her. It felt like a horrible thing to be doing. So, I told her I didn't think it was a good idea to have sex "one last time". I couldn't, was too upset. A line. I kissed her forehead, which was probably much worse than not kissing her at all. I gave her my set of keys, checked both my mail and my 'mail,' then rode my bike to the train, leaving it unlocked since I had no further use for it.

Over the next six months, I had an unbelievable amount of success in my career. I bypassed multiple levels that Canadian artists typically need to pull themselves through sweating and heaving. I went from selling every piece of mine in a group show to a cartoonishly eccentric billionaire patron, to then selling every new painting I made to the same man. I had a solo show in Toronto two days before my flight out West, and I already had two solo shows in New York lined up over the next six months. I was also in discussion with a Swiss gallery. At that age, twenty-eight, the idea of a gallery in Switzerland signaled to my unexperienced mind a life of success, ease and unending money. I've since been brutally disabused of that fantasy. Back then, however, I wasn't lying when I told you I would have no problem bringing you to Canada and eventually supporting you and your two children. I was high on a drug which has very little potency and a short half-life.

Success.

The next time we spoke I was living in a cottage heated by a wood-burning stove in the Chinatown area of Vancouver. I had nothing to hide anymore. The last time I'd seen Anna was at my art opening, where all I could think about was you. She was out of my life completely now.

My dealer informed me that because of his advances and advertising and framing costs, I'd only made four-hundred dollars out of that show.

That was the first and last time I let myself get scammed by an art dealer.

I started to realize the things I'd promised about bringing you to see me were perhaps grandiose. I became reacquainted with reality, and as is the case each time that happens, I found myself terribly disappointed and ill at ease.

My success thrived on paper but not in my bank account. Once I was set up in Vancouver and had bought the supplies I needed to make paintings for those upcoming shows, I had very little money left. Being Canadian, I immediately applied for as many grants as possible. My mother had given me a laptop as a parting gift and I used it to chat with you obsessively. I bought a cell phone with calling cards from the crack addict supply store. Every corner store in my neighborhood was a crack addict supply store. I'd talk to you at night while I painted, but the mornings were no good anymore because of the new time difference.

The first thing I noticed out west was that the birds were bigger. The mountains were shocking, but soon they became something I didn't notice anymore. I took the ocean for granted, which was only six blocks from my house, and didn't check it out until years later. Once I saw it, I didn't get the appeal. I didn't understand the value in laying down to stare at an endlessly lapping field of water. I didn't like sand in my shoes.

You didn't like your husband, but you still had him. As much as you hated him, you had him. You knew I needed to have sex and you assured me it would be fine if I did. You told me you would probably like hearing about it.

You did not like hearing about it.

I discovered by fluke a text messaging option on my phone. This was in 2002. Whenever I thought of you I sent you a text message, and I thought of you often. One day my mother called, angry at me, which was unusual.

"What are these 'text messages'?" she asked.

I said I didn't know. A thing I found on my phone.

"Well it's eight-hundred dollars for almost three-hundred of them in a month. You need to stop doing it, I can't afford that and neither can you."

I was letting my mother pay my phone bill, but I believed I was going to be able to take care of you and your family.

I was painting portraits of Winona Ryder during her shoplifting trial over and over, and the bon-vivant billionaire back home kept sending me checks for them. I could easily have had at least *your* airfare a month after I'd arrived in Vancouver, but no matter how strong my feelings for you, I'd known drugs longer, and they'd never let me down.

Hannah, loneliness, drugs, loneliness, drugs, Hannah, drugs. I saw I would never be able to bring you to me. I told you every day that soon I would be able to bring you to me. I told you I'd applied for a Canada Council grant, and once I got the ten thousand dollars, we'd book your flight. I pinned my hopes on the sudden influx, and since I'd been experiencing so much success, I felt absolutely certain I would receive the grant.

I did not receive the grant.

I told you I was still waiting for the results.

You fucked someone who worked at your school. I felt disappointed and frustrated. You emailed me new pornographic photos of yourself; your body looked ghostly, underwater somehow, or seen through a piece of gauze. They didn't do what the office slut pictures had done. I thought of *Back to The Future*, and the vanishing family photograph of the boy who was lost in the past. You were becoming not-present, not-future; you were becoming a memory I interacted with daily. I tried to make you bright and shiny, but I could only get you halfway visible.

One day my best friend in Vancouver, Jonny, told me about a birthday party he was going to and beseeched me to come. There was a woman he liked who was going to be there, and I'd apparently been spending too much time alone. I wasn't alone, I had you; but he didn't know about you, nobody did. I was starting to feel like the guy you fucked once had you much more than I did, and I'd been talking to you daily for almost a year. I was growing resentful.

So I agreed to party.

When we got there I went in to use the bathroom and say hello, then claimed a couch on the porch for the rest of the night, pissing over the railing and drinking out of my endless satchel of alcohol. A woman showed up about an hour after I did. I watched as she tried to drunkenly dismount and park her bicycle. She was beautiful. I watched her body frustrate her intentions, and occasionally her underwear became visible as she tried to lift her leg off her bike. She was wearing tights that ended just above her knees and a short white leather skirt. It turned out that flashes of underwear in real life were far more arousing than flashes frozen by a camera and mailed to me from miles away.

The woman on the bike was a tall, blonde, prom queen type. She did all that maneuvering while holding an open, full bottle of wine in one hand, which impressed me. As she moved towards the house she saw me on the couch, and without even peeking inside she came and sat next to me. She took my cigarette out of my mouth and started smoking it. I had to ask for it back.

I'd only ever been with women like me: disenchanted nascent intellectuals, outcasts, abused by parents or strangers, unhappy frowners. This woman seemed happy. I'd never seen that before. Her name was Lee. She called me "fresh meat." She told story after story, not once asking me a question.

I spent the rest of the party on the couch with her, and at the end of the night, Jonny told me to walk her home. I already was planning to. Then he told me the birthday party we were at was for her. She'd never once gone in. There was a cake for her, Happy Birthday Lee, twenty-eight candles. Apparently, the girls inside didn't even know she'd shown up and was sitting with me in the dark—they were pissed off at her.

Hearing it was her birthday, I instantly decided I should be with her, for a night or for good, whatever she'd allow. While I walked her home, I realized I hadn't thought about you once during the six or seven hours we'd been sitting together.

Back at her place I saw she had impeccable style and taste,
something I didn't know if you had. She smoked joint after joint
like a chain-smoker does cigarettes. She was visibly nervous, and
I got off on that. She told me I should go home, because she
didn't want to "do anything stupid."

Before I left she went into her bedroom and brought back
a Polaroid. It was her at a Halloween party, wearing only jeans
with the ass cut out, a reference to the obscure movie *So Fine*
with Ryan O'Neal. Her ass was beautiful and white as a bed
sheet, with a heart-shaped mole on the left cheek. She also gave
me her business card, which was just her name and phone number; no information about her ostensible business.

For reasons unknown to me I didn't call her. I wanted to but
didn't. At some point she got tired of waiting and decided to
just come to my house. When I opened the door, she was wearing an absurdly tight t-shirt that had "Immaculate Conception"
printed on it.

Within fifteen minutes I'd come in her mouth and had my
middle finger all the way up her ass while she made endearing
sounds and looked down at me between her legs, smiling. She
said she could do a trick and squeezed her nipple, squirting faux-
breast milk in my face, then she jumped blushing onto the bed.
After that I spent a record twenty-nine consecutive days with her.
My roommate thought I'd moved out. We didn't leave the bed
except to nourish and hydrate ourselves.

I'm a very simple man. I was in love.

She had some job I didn't understand, and when she'd leave
for it I'd call you to talk. You knew something was up. I wasn't
as available as I'd once been. I lied again and pretended it was
something else. When I talked to you, I was also pretending. I
decided to tell you I hadn't gotten the grant, but pretended I'd

just found out. You were crushed. I felt awful for falling in love with Lee.

Lee was never sad or angry. She seemed happy to just be alive. She wasn't pretentious or interested in what I did. She never once asked me if I thought she looked good. She was confident and funny and spontaneous. All of this was new to me, and, being young and simple-minded, I mistook that newness for love. I thought of you stuck on the other side of the world, your kids a ransom against your freedom, tethered to a piece of shit husband. I thought of your parents-in-law and how I'd be letting them down. I thought of what it would take to keep lying to you. Then I told you that I'd met someone I really liked.

You cried. I apologized. You said "Fuck off" and your accent had never sounded thicker, more fightingly Glaswegian.

The next time I called I got the machine.

Then I only ever got the machine.

Then I stopped calling.

The first time I told Lee I loved her, she said that was nice. She had an ex-boyfriend she had lived with for a year in, of all places, Australia. I hated him because he was her ex, because he was ten years older than her, and primarily, because he was a guitar player whose band was on a label I really liked.

One night a few months after that brutal first I love you, Mick, as all Australian men are called, was in town, on tour with his band. Lee said she was going to meet him for dinner. At this point I was living with her and her roommates, both of whom hated me and made it clear I wasn't welcome there alone. Lee told me she'd be done at eleven and to meet her at the restaurant, so I hung out at a friend's place and waited. I called her at eleven and she didn't pick up. I went back to my friend's place. I called her half a dozen times until my friend wanted to sleep and asked me to leave.

I walked down to the restaurant. It was approaching three in the morning. When I got closer I saw Lee out front, smiling and drunk, waving to a figure disappearing in the distance.

"Oh! You just missed Mick, I wanted you two to meet!" she slurred, drunk.

She gave a half-assed apology about being so late, catching up and all that. Such a long time and so on. And Mick's band is doing so good! Did you know there's two songs about me on the last album?

I looked at the ground and walked towards home. She was having trouble walking, I was having trouble generally. She decided to walk through an alley, and we stopped at some point and started kissing. Then suddenly she said, "Brad I love you! I love Brad Phillips!"

It felt like a punch in the face. Of any time to say it, she'd truly picked the very worst. I accused her of waiting to see if Mick wanted to be with her, if he'd be willing—the irony is not lost on me—to fly her back to Australia and take care of her. When he hadn't offered her that, I was the next best thing.

I did not like being the next best thing.

So we kicked her roommates out and we committed to each other. The first year it was fun and felt like love, and four years later we got married. Years after that, it dawned on me that it was really only good until the night before she said I love you, and the rest of it had been so slow-motion I couldn't see it; a snail's pace slide into a romance toilet.

You emailed me eight months after we'd last spoke. You weren't mad. You told me you'd been Googling me and were following my career. You told me about what you were doing, how the kids were. You'd gotten a new job in animation, which had always been your dream. We talked occasionally by email, every six months or so. You never told me about your personal life and

I never asked. You didn't ask about mine and I didn't want to tell you. I was happy to have you as a friend, but I was also increasingly dissatisfied with my marriage and began to re-romanticize you, thinking it could work. My life with Lee had begun to stink of Fleetwood Mac, incense and bullshit. I asked you once if any part of you still wanted to be with me, and that email exchange ended immediately.

The last email from you came June 17th, 2008, nine years ago this week.

You told me that you'd gotten a promotion, and were planning to move the kids out into your own place. You were going through legal hoops to get citizenship and were no longer beholden to Paul. I was happy for you and told you so.

But you never wrote back.

Just after Christmas of 2011, I got an email from your parents-in-law. I'd been trying to contact you on and off, but your email bounced back. I put ads on Craigslist very much like this, only quite a bit shorter. No information about you ever came back to me.

When Nancy and Mark wrote me, I was grateful to hear from anyone connected to you. The subject line said, "Dearest Brad," which spooked me right off the bat. I have it saved somewhere on an old hard drive, but from what I remember the first line was "We're both so terribly sad to inform you, knowing how much Hannah meant to you and you to her, but"—I must have sat in that chair for two hours, reading that email over and over.

You had died in a car accident. Paul had custody of the children. It happened in June of 2008, but your in-laws couldn't remember my last name for years, then found a letter from me to you in a box that was hidden in their garage.

At first I was crushed, truly heartbroken. But then I put it all together, and it made perfect sense.

*

Of course you'd fake your death in an attempt to get away from Paul. Maybe something had happened during the process of filing for custody or citizenship. I know Paul had a bad temper and sometimes he beat you up. I watch a lot of movies, and in movies when someone goes missing, the police often say that there are people who want to get lost and that that's not a crime. In the movies you're screaming in your head at the cops that no, that's bullshit, she's been kidnapped, nobody just vanishes.

But people do just vanish. In so many ways. Faking their death is one of them.

You were standing up to the father of your children for the first time. You were showing Paul, someone who'd never gotten anywhere in this world and still lived with his parents, that you, the daughter of a psychopath and a schizophrenic, could get ahead with some hard work and discipline. It must have been unbearable for him. I can see him now, having called in "sick" to work, laying on his couch, watching American television shows about paternity tests and goth-teen makeovers, drinking one cheap beer after the other, slowly becoming more and more angry. He would have been nearing fifty that year, and you forty-seven—ages where typically people realize it's too late to fix their lives. He'd forever be a drunk, bald, malingering construction worker, while you were defying nature, moving forward, getting better, creating a new life for yourself instead of slouching into hopelessness and apathy.

So he tried to kill you. But he was too drunk and uncoordinated. Maybe he got you good in the head, enough to make you really bleed, then passed out. Drunks like him and moments like that are easy enough to manipulate. If you called his parents and told them this was your chance to get away they would probably have helped you.

If I remember correctly your father-in-law Mark worked in

the meat industry. I've learned from movies that a pig can pass for a dead human being if they've been killed in a fiery crash.

I can see Mark and Nancy helping you pack your things. Mark taking a midnight run to the abattoir to fetch a fake dead daughter-in-law. I can see them putting it in the driver's seat, leaving some of your blood in the car; the three of you driving it to a bend in the road, getting out and putting a brick on the gas pedal. I can see you saying goodbye to yourself, and I can imagine how liberating that would have felt. A car driven by a pig, plowing through a cheap barrier and plummeting off a cliff, exploding at the bottom as they always do in movies. I can see you kissing your kids on the forehead, whispering into their ears that you'd be back for them. It must be horrible to know that he has them. I can imagine you now, struggling at some job in Poland or Norway, trying to save the money to get them to you, to start a life completely free of your past.

I understand why you did it. I understand why you had to die.

Maybe you'll see this. I hope you will. Maybe Nancy and Mark will, and pass on my message. You really have done an incredible job of vanishing. But I know you. I know you're still Googling me, and I know you're still proud.

I'll keep trying. I'll post these ads in various cities worldwide. You can trust me to be discreet, now that I know what happened. It can be another secret only we share.

I'm in love now. Much differently than ever before. This time it's real, I can feel it. Her name is Audrey. If you ever wanted me to be happy, then take comfort in knowing I am now. I've told Audrey all about you, and she's grateful to you for what you showed me so long ago.

My 'career' is still the same, I'm always popping up like someone physically incapable of drowning. I'm not rich and I'm not the kind of famous I used to think I'd be, but I don't want that fame now. I've sampled it and retched.

What I do have now is money. It's beautiful to be back home in Toronto, beautiful like all of Canada. I've been sober five years. I'm sorry that I kept that part of my life from you before, and that it stopped us from being together.

I was thinking that, wherever you are, you're probably tired and could use a vacation. I know that any money you're making you need to save so you can send for your kids. I can make you a promise now I won't break: if you want to come visit, I can buy you a return ticket. We have a big couch in our living room that you can sleep on. All I want is to finally meet you.

I'm a lot saner than I used to be. My mind is very rational now. I'm not unpredictable. I don't have delusions anymore.

I play Scrabble every day at isc.ro. My handle is Oprah. If you're drawn to more clandestine modes of communication, find me there. I spend hours a day anagramming words. Just now I realized your first name is one.

hannaH. Hannah.

PROPOSAL FOR A MEDICAL MEMOIR

psy·cho·so·mat·ic
/ˌsīkōsə'madik/
adjective

(of a physical illness or other condition) caused
or aggravated by a mental factor such as internal
conflict or stress.

A MAN SUFFERS A TERRIBLE BURN ON HIS RIGHT ARM. *IT HAP-pens after shooting up. He nods off and a dropped cigarette lights the carpet up. The flames reach their way to the crib where the baby sleeps. An alarm wakes him. His arm screams in unknown pain. The baby is gone because there was no baby, because the crib was stolen from the abandoned house during a B&E two days previous and he thought he could sell it for dope. Nothing else in the house seems to have wanted to burn, so he goes back to sleep. The next day waking up needing to score he realizes his arm is quite horrible to look at and still frighteningly painful. Walking down the block to where his dealer lives, he sees a house on fire. He runs inside. Two parents are dead in one room, overdosed, the fire crawl-ing towards corpses. In the other room, untouched by fire, a toddler is squirming on a carpet. He remembers people buy babies. He walks toward the unscorched room, picks the baby up and walks outside. An ambulance pulls up just as he exits the front door. This is an opportunity. Some people spend their lives not doing one good thing. Some of these people are bad people. Some are not. As soon as the paramedic locks eyes with the junkie, the narrative forms, and his face contorts to match the emotions required for the story. I've saved this baby, look at my arm. I almost got burnt up. Both baby and junkie are taken into the ambulance. He is shocked by the accuracy of the story that comes out of his mouth while the paramedic tends to his burns. Not all addicts are victims. Not all of them know trauma. Imagine this man did, had endured unspeakable things. Things that only drugs helped soothe.*

More than anything in this world, trauma has been the source
behind the greatest acts of transformation and creativity.

I am not attempting to be dramatic when I tell this story. I'm not
the person who says, "Life is horrible". I'm also not necessarily
saying this is a story about me. It could just as easily be one of
those "Listen Doc, my friend has this rash" type of stories: a kind
of fiction.

My first diagnosis was born. This theory only applies if you
believe, as many do, that our recent iteration of homo sapi-
ens are an aberration, a virus. The repercussions of this initial
diagnosis have been vast and complex. It is the umbrella under
which all of my other illnesses fall.

I am going to list them now.

My mental illnesses, for which I have been certified perma-
nently disabled by the government (incurable and therefore given
money to cover my rent, food and medication every month) are
structured hierarchically. I only learned of this hierarchy recently.
This is not a pity list. I am not looking to mark myself as a cliché,
though it is fine that I am one.

I have Post Traumatic Stress Disorder. I have other things,
but those things are not separate from my PTSD, as I'd previously thought. Instead, as I've recently learned, those 'other
things' are the maudlin children of my PTSD. The family tree
develops as follows: PTSD, Bipolar Disorder, then following that
in a flurry come Generalized Anxiety Disorder, Obsessive Com-
pulsive Personality Disorder, Panic Disorder with Agoraphobia,
and Impulse Control Disorder. I saw my chart when I shouldn't
have during the time I was auditioning to be legally disabled. It
listed, as the even more sickly *grandchildren* of PTSD, Polysub-
stance Addiction and Ethanol Abuse (now in remission).

For very many years I was not 'clean'. I was classically self-medicating. I've joked at 'special meetings' that if my mother knew the things I'd put up my nose, she wouldn't have given me such a hard time about that finger as a child. I used to take innumerable medications for these disorders, and now I only take one, which I will never stop taking, because life without it would mean life inside a room I never leave, garbage bags over the windows, not eating, rarely sleeping. That drug is Clonazepam, or as I refer to it sometimes, Saint Clonazepam. Or tenderly, on a moonlit night, Pam. I'm not asking for sympathy. I'm not, as some people do, boasting about how mentally ill I am. I don't feel proud of it and I don't feel sorry for myself. I just accept it as being fundamentally a part of who I am, and the reason for some of my behaviors and predilections.

I've never experienced an unbothered, medically-different mind; I don't remember a self unlike this one. Like someone born blind, I do not miss the color green. I don't like to think about the labels that describe my mental frailty. I just recognize that I'm mentally ill. The different names mean nothing to me. The meaning is in the symptoms. Those I can try and address as they appear. Were I to think of all the syndromes and disorders that manipulate me, I'd feel weighed down by the heaviness of them all. It's become healthier for me to just be watchful; observe symptoms arise when I can, then use tools I've learned to try to control how much I let those symptoms damage me or others. Part of what I've learned is to ask someone close to me, to ask my wife Cristine, to tell me when I'm acting unusual. I'm a bipolar person right now, typing this, and I'm okay. But if I started to talk a mile a minute, if I started to say grandiose things, I wouldn't recognize it happening. So, Cristine tells me. Then I know.

I'd become sad were I to count the moments that might add up to months, where I've looked at the face of someone looking back at me—a wife, a friend, family, strangers, social workers—and I knew the look that they were offering me only manifested itself when encountering the mentally ill. A combination of faux-friendliness, (perhaps even real) sympathy, "you're normal, I'm looking at you like you're normal," touched sadness, kind eyes; all of these looks are simply muscles moving to create a mask composed of moral instincts that in truth is simply hiding fear. The smiling face of the afraid. I've become so used to this face, and have thought about it at such length, that I almost return it, because I feel badly for the person looking at me, knowing I'm ill, fearing what I may do, wanting me to not feel stigmatized. They try so hard, really, they do try.

The list of physical ailments I suffer from isn't as fun, but it's necessary.

Complex Regional Pain Syndrome, or Reflex Sympathetic Dystrophy (hereafter referred to as CRPS or RSD), colloquially known in the pain community as "The Suicide Disease"—the world's most painful chronic pain disorder. A disorder I developed a week before my father died and which got worse a week after. Please, no sympathy. That's not why I'm telling you. I mention the term Suicide Disease because...well, it's obviously a good alternate term, and the rest will come later. My CRPS was triggered at age twenty by Brachial Neuritis, a term which describes a pinched nerve that, instead of healing, forever sends out pain signals.

I've also been told I have Fibromyalgia, which may be bullshit, a basket diagnosis into which undiagnosable pain/psychiatric combinations tend to get tossed. They used to call it Chronic Fatigue Syndrome, and it would get made fun of on the Phil Donahue Show.

A touch of Spina Bifida Occulta (the Pete Best of Spina Bifidas).

Chronic Costochondritis, also known as Tietze's or Slipping

Rib Syndrome. Arcane as St. Vitus' Dance, it means the connective tissue between my spine and one specific rib is weak, causing that pitiful bone to dislocate spontaneously. It was generated by a dramatic growth spurt. When it first began, I was nineteen and the pain was horrifying. Thankfully now the nerve endings at my rib head have been ground away, and it's just mildly uncomfortable. It used to dislocate if I sneezed, fucked, coughed, laughed, stood the wrong way (I've discovered there are wrong ways to stand, but have not yet learned which ways they are). A pain in my chest like a heart attack, I could only lay in one specific position for up to two weeks. I'd hear the rib clicking against its estranged partner, which had moved away like you do from a smelly man on the subway.

My girlfriend, when I got sick, was an angel about it. While I was incapacitated, she'd light my cigarettes and pour Coca-Cola in my mouth. This disease mirrors an anxiety attack, so at nineteen I first began to hear "it's all in your head." The rare and difficult to diagnose CRPS leads most physicians to say the same thing. So what I heard most often over those thirteen years, from innumerable specialists and doctors, was that "it's all in your head." I'd become enraged by those five words, knowing I was in real and spectacular physical pain.

The litany of psychiatrists I saw offered no opinion on my physical problems, but did tend to agree I was "addicted" to my own suffering.

It was a *difficult time.*

Today at forty-three, I've come to understand very differently what it means to have physical pain be "all in my head." It is still a difficult time, but compared to twenty years ago, it's a birthday party on Christmas Eve.

Although I know people with birthdays near Christmas say it's a drag.

They need to grow up.

*

What I learned from seeing my charts, from Kirk Evans, Chief of Psychiatry at Vancouver General Hospital, are the following: Usually one illness is the matriarch (The Big Mother for me was my birth, the clatter, mucus and fluorescence accompanying the unspeakable trauma of being born); then come the psychiatric and physical ailments (The Little Mother of all my psychiatric ailments is Post Traumatic Stress Disorder). The Little Mother of my physical ailments is that I'm tall and wasn't meant to be. It goes further than that though, into a nefarious and little understood region of suffering.

My physical illnesses are *somatoform*.

Liberating, embarrassing, true and bizarre, is that in fact, much of my suffering, both physical and psychiatric, truly *is* "all in my head."

Somatoform disorders are little understood and not well known, even amongst most physicians, which is why being diagnosed with one takes so long, why the somatoform sufferer will generally wear on the nerves of her general practitioner, and why patients will hear it's all in their heads without further explanation. In the argot of the burnt out ill-informed physician, "it's all in your head" is synonymous with hypochondria. Hypochondria though is simply a component of any anxiety disorder. Being called a *malingerer* however implies a hypochondria that is conscious—you want attention, you seek it, you make up ailments. These are interesting grey areas in medicine and psychology. Munchausen Disorder involves making oneself sick for attention, while Munchausen by Proxy is making someone else sick, typically one's own child, with hopes of eliciting attention. Often Munchausenites are more informed about contemporary illness than their physicians, and can mimic expertly a variety of complex or obscure diseases. Like the pseudo-heroic, the baby-saving crack addict, Munchausen by proxy involves a person seeking acclaim or sympathy for their vigilance/suffering.

An example: my daughter's heart almost stopped beating (because I poisoned her), but I'm such a good mother I noticed it right away and brought her here to the emergency room (to be complimented on my good parenting).

Autobiography is Munchausen by proxy.

Somatoform disorders are none of these while often being mistaken for them. This is why I pointed out that the colloquial term for CRPS is The Suicide Disease, not for attention like a malinger or Munchausenite, but because it points to a direct line between the mind and body; a suffering shared by both that creates an internal language within a human being in pain.

If you suffer from a somatoform disorder, as much as you will be in horrific pain, or blind, or deaf, you are suffering from a mental illness.

The CRPS sufferer, if they are somatoform, is experiencing indescribable pain in their bodies because they aren't prepared to mentally process trauma from their past. Instead of committing suicide because of their mental suffering, they will commit suicide to put a stop to the unceasing, untreatable pain they feel in nerve clusters. In the end, they've still committed suicide to put an end to their mental trauma. This is the obscure internal language within the body, directing a limb to utilize a tool to end pain in one place which echoes from another. The somatoform patient who commits suicide is a puppet of their own subconscious.

Somatoform disorders are physical ailments of typically just a few types: blindness, deafness, paralysis, or chronic pain. Each manifestation, again, is the result of unprocessed psychological pain. A person who goes completely deaf will see an audiologist, and the tests will show no signs of hearing loss, but the patient genuinely cannot hear a single sound.

(When I was initially injured and pinched my nerve, I was given nerve conduction tests which resulted in the diagnosis of Brachial Neuritis. I had a genuine, technologically-confirmed nerve disorder. Years later, when the pain in the same area was far worse, I was diagnosed visually and by touch with CRPS. For confirmation I was sent to a neurologist, and all electromyography and nerve conduction tests performed produced no evidence to support my still being in terrible pain. These were the same tests that produced my initial diagnosis of Brachial Neuritis. The doctor administering the tests was astonished when I couldn't feel the large needle being inserted into my atrophied shoulder. Muscle atrophy and complete dermal numbness are also symptomatic of CRPS).

The paralyzed patient will be subject to a battery of tests, each indicating there is no evidence they shouldn't be able to walk around; yet they will be completely unable to move, will shit themselves, need breathing and feeding tubes, and their muscles will atrophy. Although some people will go through a lot to get the attention they need, very few will sit in their own cold shit while their body wastes away, faking that they cannot swallow food or use their lungs properly.

The Suicide Disease, RSD, CRPS, began at a time in my life when I was suffering much more from mental illness.

The initial injury was typical. I was a courier, I pinched a nerve from a heavy bag, I developed brachial neuritis. In almost all cases, this nerve damage will correct itself. But while I was waiting for that nerve damage to heal, my father died very suddenly and in a shocking way, with my last words to him having been "Go fuck yourself." In the weeks after his funeral, not only did the pain in my shoulder not abate, it worsened.

I developed chronic costochondritis, Slipping Rib disorder, in my late teens. It was the result of an extraordinary growth spurt. This is a genuine ailment unconnected to my mind. Chronic costochondritis does not fall under the umbrella of somatoform disorders. It's a simple mechanical ailment caused by overtaxed ligaments.

However, being unusually short for most of my formative years—including through junior and much of high-school (making me a target for bullies and mockery)—did cause me to suffer mentally. In the tenth grade, I was four feet ten inches and weighed seventy-four pounds. I was noticeably unlike everyone else—a weak, frangible, target. I prayed all that year to a God I didn't believe in to grow taller. I prayed throughout the entire summer between grades ten and eleven. When school started in September, I'd managed to squeak above five feet and was hovering around one hundred pounds. This small improvement had no effect on the bullies who welcomed me back to school with beatings and verbal abuse.

I left school a month into grade eleven. Not because of the bullying—I'd become use to that—but because nascent mental illnesses were proving themselves to be more than I could handle. Particularly anxiety, agoraphobia and depression. I spent the rest of that year inside my mother's house, never venturing outside. My sister would bring my school work to me. I continued to pray I'd grow taller. I don't remember exactly what month it was that I woke up in the night with intense pain in my legs and arms, but I knew what it was, so I had my aunt bring me a cross that I wore discreetly under my shirt. I kept praying. I kept growing. By the time grade twelve approached, able to return to school and numbingly medicated for my mental issues, I was six foot two and one hundred and fifty pounds.

Not a somatoform disorder. Very much a physiological disease, obviously rooted in the musculoskeletal state of my beleaguered body. However, without the agonizing torment of bullies which lead me to reach out to a God I didn't believe in for assistance, it's possible I may never have become as tall as I am now. Not because of the divine intervention of a beneficent God, but because mind over matter is real; real the way my mother caused the tumor in her breast to shrink and vanish by repeatedly envisioning it disappearing.

Doctors today put a great deal of stock in the ability we have to shape and alter our bodies through the power of our minds. It's almost become mainstream in medicine for cancer patients, in concert with chemotherapy, to be told that they should meditate and visualize their tumors shrinking. In this way then, my slipping rib, although not specifically somatoform, is nonetheless a syndrome I live with whose source I can trace to mental calamity I suffered as a young person. I sought relief and received it. Be careful what you wish for. All clichés are true.

In 1993 James Breslin wrote a biography of Mark Rothko. Rothko made paintings that people, whether I agree or not, find terribly sad and tragic. I see beautiful colors and shapes. Undeniable though are the shapes he sliced into his wrists and the colors that poured out of those incisions. Those shapes and colors were objectively sad and tragic. In his book, Breslin discusses Rothko's penchant for lying and exaggerating when describing his life in Russia before he and his family emigrated to America. He told people his family had narrowly escaped Stalin's pogroms, along with other tales of woe and misery. Breslin, through research, found many of these stories to be untrue. Rothko, who genuinely did suffer from clinical depression, required a false past to elicit the level of sympathy he needed from his friends, a level of sympathy to sooth and match the suffering he endured daily in his mind. It's easy to dismiss your whining depressed friend. It's harder to dismiss your whining depressed friend if they convince you that the depression they're whining about was caused by world-renowned atrocities. Rothko lied because he needed more attention and understanding from those around him than he would've been able to elicit if he'd just been himself—a clinically depressed alcoholic. This is a kind of malingering. Rothko was a verbal Munchausenite, concocting tales that would garner him the "Oh Mark, poor thing" that he needed.

There is no one more manipulative than the depressed person.

The sick person runs a close second, but who can blame them? Or at least blame them out loud. The mentally ill are the invisibly sick, and it's much easier to castigate someone with a hidden wound than someone with a pustulating one.

Listening to myself describe being sick is sort of nauseating, redolent of drama. It may be a stretch, but I think I can sell the hypothesis that my pathetic, cowardly little rib, always seeking solace in safer regions of my body, can be traced to mental suffering. Get bullied, it hurts, pray to grow, grow, body says no, rib goes pop. Roll credits.

Utilizing the osmotic knowledge I've gained throughout being a sick person, I believe that my CRPS developed because I was unable to process both my father's suicide and the fraught state of our relationship at the time. Instead of healing emotionally with the help of a therapist or a book on grieving, I swallowed that pain and never expelled it. When it found a nerve cluster as active as a Berlin disco, the pain decided to chill out there. I then began to undergo a complex transformation from physical to mental illness, all the while unaware of what was happening.

What if the last thing I'd said him to him was "I love you" instead of "Go fuck yourself"? I've thought about it. I've thought about it for his sake, not simply as a choose-your-own-medical-adventure medical path not taken. Harsh words, the last ones spoken to a dead loved one, are always bad news. Though if they knew those *were* my last words to him, none of his acquaintances would have thought me out of line. Nonetheless, regret consumed me, and I still feel it now. To this day I'm unsure whether my distress is rooted more in what I last said to him, or how he died. Even though my father gave me very little besides Post Traumatic Stress Disorder, I still wish I'd been the kinder of two men and forgiven him.

For months after he died, I'd often imagine his final moments, and although he rarely showed any sign that he thought of me, I began to imagine that my "go fuck yourself" played through his mind constantly before he killed himself. Really, it's not logical. It doesn't suit our relationship or his personality. But death does this—skews perception, generates endless replays and fantasy scenarios. In all likelihood, he was doing what he'd always done when he decided to die. Which is to say whatever the fuck he wanted, while giving no consideration to how his actions might affect others. I'm not being judgmental here. (I have no right to be judgmental). That there was no note, that my sister and I received nothing (not that there would have been much to receive that would've been legal), these things and more, both then and now, confirm that he was indulging himself one last time.

The "go fuck yourself" had been instigated when I encountered him on the subway a year before, drunk at eleven in the morning, unable to recognize his only son when I stood in front of him and said –

"Hi Dad."
"What?"
"It's me. Remember me? I saw you in the hospital at Christmas. You were handcuffed to the bed."
"[Unintelligible]"
"Brad. Your son. You're B____ Phillips. I know you."

"You have any money? Gimme money."

"You look like shit"

"*You* look like shit. Money"

"Go fuck yourself, Dad."

When I replay it in my mind, I sit beside him. Although I was poor then, I give him whatever spare change I have in my pocket. I put my arm around him. I gently try to remind him of who I am, who he is, who we are to each other. Even though it doesn't work, when my stop comes I put my mouth in his ear and whisper "I love you," then kiss his cheek and get off the subway.

Absolutely absurd. The abnegation of self required to enact a scene like this just isn't in my character. I should forgive myself. The doctors have all said this. Forgiveness is the first step to recovery. I did not. I have not.

I'd endured outrageous trauma while being raised by someone who shouldn't have had children. I knew though that it wasn't my fault. Unlike other children raised in similar environments, I never once entertained the idea that I was guilty or that I deserved it. However, my youthful self-awareness didn't help me to escape without Post Traumatic Stress Disorder and a crippling anxiety problem. After my father's death, it wasn't being dangled off the roof of a high-rise that haunted me daily, it was that I'd told him to go fuck himself, and that he'd then committed suicide. In my mind for many years, this was a truly cruel thing I'd done. Laughable in comparison to the cruelty inflicted on me. Had my car flown off the road, bursting into flames at the bottom of a cliff, simply because I'd finally grown so tired of being cut off on the highway that I resorted to giving someone the finger? Because I was and am that car. That explosion. That finger.

*

My daily life is plainly factual and full of things I know are true. I know each day I take 180 milligrams of M-Eslon (slow release morphine) and 10 milligrams of Nortriptyline. I know every night I must drink a chalky mouthful of Milk of Magnesia to combat the chronic constipation I endure due to my enormous opiate dosage, and I know every night I take 100 milligrams of Trazodone without which I would never sleep. I know each day I take six milligrams of Clonazepam without which I know I would be paralyzed. I know that I have hyperhidrosis from both the Morphine as well as from the Nortriptyline. I know that I struggle to maintain a healthy weight because I sweat off every calorie I consume while sleeping. I know that my anxiety disorder is exacerbated by the unpredictability of my gastrointestinal system, the aforementioned laxative either working too well or not well enough, so that I never feel the sense of excremental satisfaction and finality that normal people feel. This anxiety about unpredictable bowel action is directly related to a single moment of abuse that took place when I was nine years old. In a car with my father driving drunk, a sudden need to go the bathroom, a refusal to pull over, loss of bowel control—introduction of fists and screaming.

Anyone who knows me well knows I do not complain about my health. By describing the ways that my body and mind are broken and ill, I am not attempting to elicit a "poor Brad" response. I simply want, both for myself and others, to learn more about how my mind sickens my body, and how my body sickens my mind. I know I'm not alone. I know that understanding what my mind and body do to each other necessarily implies that my body can heal my mind and my mind can heal my body. I suppose in writing this I hope to find others like me, and assure them they are not alone. That maybe together we can learn to heal. That recognizing being told "it's all in your head" is not always an insult, but on occasion may even be empowering.

But inside of me lives an ouroboros of anxiety, trauma, illness and medication. Constantly asserting its presence in my daily life, I'm far too much under its control. Hypnotized by symptoms and sources, I'm still in no position to heal myself based on what I've learned. While I claim empowerment as an option, it's evaded me, and as I write this I do so as a person who's still very sick.

What I know today is that it's all in my head and it's all in my body. It's both places at once, equally formidable wherever I encounter it. If I still my body or engage it, find restive moments or active ones, the mind flares up. If I rest my mind or engage it, be wholly present or decamp to the future, my body flares up to remind me I'm trapped inside of it. What I know at my age, having spent more than half my life with ailments both physical and mental, is that my only solution is the one I learned while I spent time in various institutions—acceptance. Acceptance is the answer to all of my problems.

THE BARISTA,
THE ROOSTER & ME

A WOMAN HASN'T SEEN HER SON FOR SIX YEARS AFTER KICK-ing him out of the house for stealing money for drugs. To deal with the loss of her son, the mother ends up finding comfort in those same drugs. One day, needing to get high, she walks to the spot where she always buys dope. Instead of her usual dealer beckoning her into the doorway of the bar, she realizes that the man taking her money is her son.

A man is in Houston on business. He hasn't had sex with his wife in over two years. He isn't the type of man to pay for sex when he travels. This time, frustration with his marriage combined with his neglected sex drive overpower his sense of morality. Flipping through the back of a free local newspaper he finds the escort ads. Hot college girls who will do anything. Fresh-faced. Greek Islands. Eating at the Y. Will wear school uniform if requested. So naive as to think the body in the photo is the body of the girl who will arrive at his door, he nervously places the call, empties half the mini-bar and waits. An hour later there's a knock at the door. He doesn't want to answer it. He's changed his mind. But that's not an option. He opens the door. It takes him more than a minute—but not her, who's begun crying—to realize the girl standing in his hotel room wearing a cheap orange dress with a neck tattoo is his daughter Alicia, who he hasn't seen since she left home to begin her sophomore year at art school.

Worried he'll be late for work and gunning for a promotion, a young father doesn't properly check his rear-view mirror, slowly reversing over his four-year old son, who is struggling to learn to ride a bike with training wheels.

Traveling to Jordan to visit a dying aunt, a chemical engineering student finds himself duct-taped to a chair in a room that exists on no maps, only six hours after landing in his homeland for the first time.

A family of four wins one-hundred-eighty million dollars in the lottery.

Taking a long train trip across the country to treat herself and relax, a recently-widowed woman is unable to sleep in her private car. She is traveling through nothing but flat, endlessly replicating prairie. She cups her hands to the window and presses her nose to the glass, attempting to get a look at what's speeding by her. After a minute, passing before her so quickly she'll spend the rest of her life questioning whether or not it truly happened, she sees a bald man in a white jumpsuit standing only a few feet from the tracks, staring into the windows. In that nanosecond, they make eye contact.

The night before I got shipped off to live with strange men for a year, Paul, one of my roommates, found me at the bottom of the stairs when he came home from the casino. I was a six-foot-tall confusion of limbs and paper white skin lying crumpled at the bottom of a staircase. My memory is fuzzy, but I remember Paul kicked me in the stomach and waited until my eyes found his. He asked if I could spare a cigarette then laughed obnoxiously and walked into the kitchen. He laughed because I was naked and obviously didn't have any cigarettes.

I felt my face and I knew something was wrong. I recalled my friend Greg peeling me off Hastings Street, insisting that I stop what I was doing.

"Just stay down. Stay down or come with me. Don't go back for more."

I remember going back for more.

I remember the sound it made inside my head when the bouncer cracked my face on the wall, breaking my orbital bone.

I remember understanding that this was why my face felt wrong. I remember being scared to look in the mirror. I don't remember how I got home, but I did.

I'd packed my bags early that morning, knowing that I only had one day left to get fucked up; one day left before I got shipped off to live with the strange men for a year. I'd had one day left and I wanted to use it. Based on my broken face, I guessed I did.

The van that came to get me had three guys in it, all of them tough-looking dummies. I remember thinking, "These guys are dummies." I remember the driver saying "Oh fuck" when he saw me. I think they carried me down the front stairs of the house and helped me into the van. One of them must have taken my bag. I remember my roommate Paul when I looked back. He gave me the finger and smiled.

Thirty days later, I knew who the dummy was.

The strange men were taking me to what people call rehab. Rehab is not what people in rehab call rehab. We call it treatment. Being in treatment was the first time I ever saw the good in men. It was a unifying environment; not only because we were all addicts, or addicts trying to get well, but because each one of us, no matter what our story, found ourselves together because of things that had happened in our lives—those things from which we could not return.

The stories I have of that year are innumerable.

The following few help me explain why today I find myself struggling so hard to deal with a problem I've been having—a problem I've been having with the sensitive barista who lives beneath my wife, Cristine, and I in a way where nobody ends up hurt, or in jail.

One story I have is about Mike. Mike was a sweet First Nations man who moved with me from the hospital to the halfway house where I lived for nine months. On weekends we were allowed to go to the community centre, where we'd all swim. It was the only time that nobody was breathing down our necks. Mike had gotten his stomach stapled years before, and it always broke my heart to see him in the pool in a loose black t-shirt. There was a sweet fat kid who would come with us who also wore a t-shirt in the pool, but with Mike I knew it was because he was ashamed of whatever his skin looked like underneath, which for some reason felt more sad to me.

Mike was always quiet. Like a lot of people I came to know that year, he would always make sure that wherever he was in a room, nobody could get behind him. It was almost funny in group therapy the way there'd be so much empty space, every single guy sitting in a chair pressed up against the wall. Prison habits are hard to break I learned.

Mike came to treatment three years after getting out of the penitentiary, where he'd spent twelve years for second-degree murder. He'd been with his two young daughters one weekend near Christmas. He took them shopping and when they exited the mall, Mike put a fresh hundred-dollar bill in a Salvation Army kettle. As he walked away, he looked back and saw the guy with the kettle carefully extract the hundred and slip it into his pocket. Mike told his daughters to wait in the car, then he took a crowbar from the floor of his back seat and slowly walked back towards the mall.

Mike said he remembered nothing, but later discovered he'd killed the guy by hitting him in the head and face with the crowbar over twenty times.

He would cry in group therapy when he told us how his daughters screamed when he came back to them covered in blood. He didn't know he was covered in blood, because he'd been blackout drunk. The police picked him up before he left the parking lot.

Another story I have is about Danny. Danny moved into our halfway house after I'd been there a while. Of everyone I met there, he was the one I felt most drawn to. Danny was a bald, fifty-year old longshoreman who'd never been clean for more than a few months since the age of nine. He laughed like a cartoon villain at inappropriate moments. He was illiterate. Outside of cleaning and going to 12 step meetings, Danny and I spent a lot of empty time in the house together, so I used some of mine to help him learn to read. Danny was sort of like a child. An insane child, but nonetheless a child.

Danny had never owned a computer before, and the house PC had blocks on it that restricted our access to porn and gambling websites.

Enter Dave, the last house manager we had. Dave, who would sometimes bring his one-legged meth-head girlfriend over on weekends to fuck in his bedroom with the door open, was far more relaxed about rules than the previous managers. Marcello, another guy in the house, had a friend who sold stolen laptops and Dave didn't care if we all had one.

Danny wanted one. I thought I could use it to help him learn to read. Danny called computers "the porn machines", and at first I thought he was kidding. I soon learned that he truly didn't know they served any other function outside of putting pornography in front of your face.

So Marcello got him a laptop and Danny opened it one night while the rest of were about to drive to an NA meeting. He looked at it and held it like a monkey might hold an hourglass. He claimed total confusion as to how it worked. Someone said, "You'll figure it out Dan." And when we got back from the meeting two hours later, there he was in the living room, placidly watching something I'd never seen before: Russian anorexic porn. I glimpsed the cock of a young comrade visibly poking up through the atrophied pelvic muscles of a far too thin girl. Someone asked Danny, "What the fuck how did you find this?" and he just shrugged. Danny had found a very dark hole online within two hours of finding the power button on the porn machine.

A week before I left, Danny got kicked out. Not for relapsing but for reorganizing Marcello's face using the heavy leg of an oak coffee table he broke off during a fight over control of the television remote.

Through research I've learned that crack addicts enjoy shows like Storage Wars and Duck Dynasty and are inveterate channel flippers, while junkies just want to watch dolphins on the Discovery Channel nonstop.

I was sitting on the pleather sofa, looking at sexual photos of myself and the girl I was seeing when Danny did it. Blood sprayed my laptop and sweater. Nobody in the house wanted to call the cops since they all had police issues, so I called, because it's a drag to watch someone die, and I've miraculously never had trouble with the law. Danny was arrested. I didn't mean for that to happen. It was the last time I saw him.

But there's another story I want to tell about Danny.

Like most longshoremen, Danny made a lot of money and was a crack and heroin addict.

Longshoremen work on call, are unionized and often corrupt, and smoke crack in their trucks collecting double time waiting for something to do. Half the people I met in rehab were either longshoremen or they worked on oil rigs. Too much free time and too much money is bad for the addict brain. Danny used to tell me a lot of stories, and I'd be crying with laughter while he'd ask me what was funny. He thought his life was normal.

A typical day for Danny when he wasn't working was to get four hookers to come to his house and be themselves. He told me the house rules were that as soon as the hookers got there, everyone had to take off their clothes. Then the crack smoking would begin in earnest. He never explained the need for nudity, but it somehow made perfect sense. The hookers were there to fuck, but that was their secondary purpose. Mostly they were there to keep Danny company. He spent more money on crack for them and himself than he did on their hourly rates, and he'd often keep them for the entire weekend. These weren't high end escorts, but he was paying out at least fifty an hour for each girl for 48 hours. Drug math indicates that that's an astonishing amount of rock cocaine.

His life sounded fun. It sounded different than the life of someone married to opiates, which rarely involves hookers. It does often involve getting naked though, but only because you're so fucking sweaty.

Danny had a parrot named Fucker. And besides dealers and hookers, Danny only had two visitors to his house—his mother and his parole officer. The parrot didn't have many words or sentences to blurt out, because neither did Danny. So his parole officer would drop in, or his mother might bring him a casserole, and Fucker would say one of two things: "Suck Dan's dick!' and "Danny wants a hoot! Danny wants a hoot!" The part that cracked me up every time wasn't just what the parrot said, but Danny doing an impersonation of a parrot mimicking his own voice.

Danny would always feel betrayed by Fucker when the PO came, because while he might be able to lie and say he'd been clean, Fucker would let his Parole Officer know that in fact Danny had been asking someone to suck his dick while he was smoking crack. Danny loved Fucker though and even though the bird got his parole revoked and upset his mom, he never spoke ill of it, and kept it until it died.

*

There is one story that Danny used to tell that has probably taught me the most of all his stories though, and it's epic.

Danny had been working eighty hour weeks for close to six months, and the only time he had to get high and sleep was when he got home at five in the morning. I don't know the bylaws of other cities, but in Vancouver and its environs, you can own chickens and roosters if you use their eggs to feed your family. Two houses down from Danny, a Chinese family owned a particularly robust rooster. Danny would get home, do a small hoot and drink a beer then try to sleep. As he described it, every single morning during those six months, the moment he'd finally settle into sleep, the rooster would start to do its thing. I wish I could type the sound of Danny doing the rooster call. It was convincing and scary. Danny was a short-tempered man to begin with, so add long hours of work and a love affair with crack cocaine, and the rooster soon became Danny's nemesis.

This rooster tested Danny's character. Then one day it pushed him too far. It got inside his head and scratched. He said it took him a lot of crack and prayer to get to the place he needed to get to on that day.

On that fated morning when he got back from work, instead of taking one hoot and trying to sleep, Danny consumed a great deal of crack and rum then took off all his clothes. The nudity is for me both the inscrutable and comic centre of the story. He got his aluminum baseball bat, sat on the edge of his bed, took hit after hit off his pipe, and waited.

Then it came.

When he told the story, at this point Danny would take the rooster sound even further, like something from Revelations. It was Dante's rooster. It was the air siren that signaled the end of the world. Who was brave enough to, instead of cowering in the cellar, leave nude through the sliding glass doors, a bat in one hand, a rum and Coke in the other?

Danny was.

He went outside. He was higher than he'd ever been. His heart beat, as he said, like 'A Africa drum' in his chest. The sun was barely up. Lights began to come on in the houses around him. Danny, in his horrible pale and pudgy nudity, began to run. Here he would defensively insist that not one drop of his drink spilled. He hopped his fence with bat and drink in hand. He hopped the other. Then there he was, man against bird. Stark naked versus glorious plumage. The bird knew something was up. Danny said it took at least twenty minutes of chasing the rooster in circles until the geometry lined up. Then with one swing, propelled by a deep energy going back to his childhood, back to why he smoked crack, in super slow motion the bat came down until it connected with the bird's head, who looked up at him with sad resignation. Danny said the head flew over the fence into the next yard, and while the body twitched, Danny cursed and taunted it. He apparently told the rooster, "Now you won't fucking coo-coo any fucking coos will you motherfucker." Then Danny returned to his home the same way he'd came; climbing the fences instead of jumping, enjoying his rum and coke. When he got home though, he walked right through his closed sliding glass doors; then got into bed bleeding, stuck with shards of glass. Animal control came an hour later, but being a lifelong addict it didn't take long for Danny to charm them into fucking off.

I imagine they were rightfully terrified.

The way Danny tells it you think the story is done there, but it isn't. Danny told us that he had always been a pariah in that neighborhood, and nobody had ever talked to him, but after silencing the beast, he said that every Christmas after that day, when he reached into his mailbox, there would be unsigned hand-delivered letters from people in the neighborhood, thanking him for what he had done.

Two stories from a year littered with them.

My hope is that they illustrate something. My year in treatment—what I witnessed, what behaviors became familiar to me—returned me to my place of birth forever changed. What transformed inside of me while there constitutes an experience from which I could not return as the Brad Phillips I once was.

People think that getting sober means getting better, becoming a better person.

Sometimes it does, but sometimes it only means getting sober.

My problem five and a half years later, now, is trivial, relative to the constellation of problems I was lost in before, but it's a problem nonetheless.

My problem is with the barista who lives underneath the apartment I share with my wife.

We moved into our apartment on December 1st. We are quiet people, Cristine and I. While she was in Florida over Christmas, I was watching a movie in bed. Then I heard a knock at my door.

It was eleven at night, and I was watching was *The Verdict* with Paul Newman. If you know this movie you know the only sound is dialogue. When I opened the door a hip twenty-something bro was standing there, his mute girlfriend beside him for support, staring at the ground. He nervously complained about the movie. He said that he had to wake up early for work. Against all instincts surging inside of me, I told him I'd turn the volume down.

He thanked me and left. A few days later, Cristine was back home and it happened again. This time I stayed in bed—her idea—knowing I would be prone to lose my temper. She spoke to him at the door and returned to me. She told me his name was Jackson. We both laughed.

Jackson styled his hair. Jackson seemed vain. But we loved our new apartment and didn't want to cause any problems, so we began to test out ways to alleviate his distress. We put the speaker on a towel. We put the speaker on a table. Over the following four months, Jackson, who Cristine had by now told to text instead of forcing her out of bed, complained at least ten more times. And each time he would mention that he started work early. We were waking him up, Cristine and I, with the speaker turned low and now on our bed, watching the notoriously bass heavy films *Dead Ringers* and *Barry Lyndon*.

Having only dealt with him that first time, I was developing some serious animosity for Jackson.

Eventually, we found the right volume and he stopped texting us for almost a month. We'd lay in bed, Cristine no longer able to rest her head on my chest as she needed both ears to strain to listen to whatever we were watching with the volume as low as we could manage.

I was not happy with this scenario.

Now my wife is again away. I'm alone, waiting, my mind imagining various scenarios. I want it to happen again.

The previous week I'd gone to the doctor. Cristine, who rarely has time alone in the house, was packing for her trip at two in the afternoon and decided, reasonably to our minds, to listen to Aaliyah with the volume turned up high. Two in the afternoon is a demilitarized zone when it comes to noise. Two in the afternoon is a free for all.

Not for Jackson.

Before the first song was even over, he texted Cristine asking her to please turn the music down. He again mentioned his early rising job, and said that he was trying to get some work done in his apartment. Before, we hadn't known what this taxing job was. Then the information arrived on her phone, strangely to my mind without shame—he told her that he and his partner were *both baristas*. I instantly wondered why he didn't just say they worked at coffee shops. So we'd been, while making art and attempting to write insightful or touching prose and editorial pieces, fucking up the life of a latte artist. No, *two* latte artists. This is why he had to wake up early. To get to the boutique coffee shop, which was across the street. When I got home Cristine was happy and showed me their conversation. We both laughed and said that the work he had to do in his apartment was probably tweaking a vocal track for the demo his band was producing.

She had held her ground though, and told him no. Suck it up, essentially.

She felt better after doing it.

But what Cristine doesn't know is I don't feel better. I feel angry. I feel pissed off that my wife—so quiet, so undemanding—wasn't even given the space to listen to one song while she packed her bag to go on what might be an emotionally difficult trip to see her family.

I want Jackson to come back.

I sit here at night, my finger hovering over the volume button on my laptop while I listen to Carpathian Forest. Because Jackson is my rooster. A reliably irritating, overly-preened nuisance with no consideration for others. Danny's stories did more than entertain me. They taught me about revenge. They taught me how to deal with the world extrajudicially.

This is the version of me that has come home. Sober yes, but not improved in all areas. In some ways, worse. I can't encase my anger in an opiate duvet. I can no longer drop it in an endless bottle of Jim Beam. So the only thing saving Jackson today, at 8:27 PM, is that Cristine and I haven't yet found a table we like enough for our apartment. We want something beautiful we'll have for the rest of our lives. That we don't yet have it is the sole reason I'm not turning up the volume tonight, waiting to answer my door, with nothing but a smile and the freshly torn off leg of our new, beautiful Edwardian table.

DUMB TIDE

PROLOGUE

One unremarkable afternoon, 2007, in the sterile Swiss city of Basel, I was 33, eating shredded carrots in the home of a family of strangers on Frobenstrasse with my ex-wife, Lee. We were there for an art exhibition. The city's art mafia had arranged for visiting artists to be put up by locals since the hotels were reserved for gallery owners and writers.

A husband, a wife, two children, male and female. We spoke no Swiss-German; they spoke no English. The husband yelled 'Compost!' and never spoke again. This afternoon after finishing my carrots I walked through the apartment into the backyard to have a cigarette in the shade. One of the children I could see at the top of the stairs was playing with a toy. The mother sat at the kitchen table, leafing through a magazine. As I walked past her she looked up at me and smiled kindly. I smiled back. Then my periphery registered the magazine. She was looking at real, horrifying hardcore child pornography. Twelve and thirteen year old kids with fat, hairy, damp men. I wish I had not looked. I could not process it. My hands shook while I tried to smoke in the backyard. I didn't want the cigarette. I wanted to tell Lee what I'd seen. Quickly I walked back the way I'd come. She sat there still, browsing through the magazine like an Ikea catalogue. She smiled up at me again as if everything was perfectly fine. Once I got into our room, I told Lee what I'd seen. She said shut up. I said no. She wanted to go see for herself. You don't need to see that for yourself, I said. I wasn't a liar, and she knew my sense of humor wasn't that dark or unhumorous. On the pretext of wanting coffee she headed for the kitchen. Seconds later I heard Lee scream. I heard another scream. I heard children scream. Lee came back in, her face was red, she was shaking and sweating. She stared at me in a way I had never seen, in a way that seemed religious. She packed our bags and dragged me to a bus. On the bus we talked about it. Had it been a man it would have been as simple to comprehend as a foul smell in a bathroom after someone walked out. This was something very different, something we couldn't process. I began to drink more after that trip, although I haven't had a drink in many years now.

1.

My job is to make paintings. I've been doing it for a long time now. Twenty years of painting for deadlines, praying for deadlines, hating the deadlines, meeting the deadlines. People with jobs say they wish they had my job. I wish I had theirs. I don't identify as a painter—the paint splattered pants, intoxicated by turpentine—painting is just the vehicle I mastered first. I also make art by writing and photography, and by manufacturing fake business cards.

All vehicles are heading in the same direction.

When you're young and declare you want to be an artist, people say, 'So you mean you don't want a real job?' But after two decades of this, I can't imagine a harder job. Coal mines, proctology, septic tank work, all unpleasant. I think I'd still take them over this. Never not working, never not thinking about working, no reason to ever stop, nobody telling you to start, no reliable paycheck, no pension, no medical. If I were the type of person to say, 'It's for the birds,' then I'd say that. Being an artist, painting, is for the birds.

I think about death a lot—the dying of it. The way it will happen, the sounds and smells I will hear and smell last. Where it will happen and how. It's normal to think about death as it gets closer. I'm forty-two. But in truth it's always close. It's no closer now than when I was five and no closer then than it will be in thirty years. I want to be gone, but not now. Not like when I was a young cliché. Now, I have reasons to stick around and see how it all plays out. How it all plays out. Imagine if I said things like that. Things playing out. *It all* playing out. My life playing out. The theatrics of days.

It seems universally accepted that the ocean and its unrelenting tide is a source of comfort and peace. The Pacific Ocean is, after all, named the Pacific. I myself find it boring. But boredom is a kind of comfort, and a modern luxury. Boredom can be pacifying. What does the ocean really do, but deliver one pre-dictable wave after another? In this way it's like life. Every morning my body wakes, crunches, shits, cries out for food. Then it aches and moves and works and tires, eats and sleeps again, setting up the same for the following morning. This is a kind of tide. It isn't calming or pacific.

Life is the same tide, the same dumb tide, everyday coming towards you predictably. Why can't I find the blasé solace in my lapping, boring life that others find when they sit on the beach?

2.

I want, when I'm dying, however it may happen, to have the opening song from the 1975 Arthur Penn film *Night Moves* playing. If I die in a hospital bed, I can ask Cristine to play it. If I fear something is amiss inside my body, I can play it in my headphones twenty-four seven. I'll have to buy headphones. Twenty-four seven. People who say that. Have I said that.

It's a lovely instrumental bit, from *Night Moves*. I don't know who wrote it. I think it suits me and my leaving this shell for whatever's next. For my funeral I have a different song, and I've had it for years. Someone close to me knows to play it.

3.

Night Moves, 1975, starring Gene Hackman and a young Melanie Griffith. She was seventeen when shooting started and eighteen when it ended. She's naked twice in the film. I'm certain cineaste pedophiles have tried to figure it out, but there's just no way of knowing if those scenes are child pornography or not. It was different back then, when Polanksi raped that girl. In the film it's addressed briefly (not the Polanski rape), although Griffith's sexuality and the way men can't help but succumb to it is present throughout. She runs away to Florida, where Hackman has been sent by her mother to track her down. Griffith's character is living with her stepfather and his 'old lady' and Hackman asks the stepfather if, you know, have you. Did you? It? Transpire? And the stepfather says, 'Harry, you talk straight'—something like that. Then he says, 'Well look at her, it should be illegal.' And Hackman says, 'It is.' Just like that. These days a movie like *Night Moves,* well those scenes, wouldn't make it to the final cut. It's beautiful the way Griffith's nascent sexuality permeates the film, yet it's broken down with such concision by that one line. 'It is.'

I watch a movie every night now when I'm done with work. Rather, when I tell myself I'm done. I'm not done, I'm on a break. Painting is absenting yourself from reality to live in the space between your eyes and your hand; so for the last three months, to exercise my brain, I've been writing reviews of the movies I watch. I write them as if I'm writing them during the period of their release. I save them to this laptop and don't look at them again.

In my review of Night Moves I discuss the films made during this period, the fuzzy ratings loophole of the 'Golden Age' of gritty American movies like *Marathon Man, Taxi Driver, Straw Dogs* etc. In my review of *Night Moves,* I discuss Griffith's character and the male lovers who Hackman harangues to glean her location as representational of the dark seventies hangover of an unrealized sixties dream. I mention Polanski raping that girl on the boat. Anjelica Huston was there. It was no big deal then. Not to Huston or Polanski that is. Child rape. Maybe it's no big deal in Hollywood still, I don't know. Cory Feldman says it is. Websites exist outing Kevin Spacey as a pedophile. I also write about the assassinations of both Kennedy brothers as they come up in the film. They stand in as exemplars of America as spoiled milk; milk being all American in some way.

I recently watched and reviewed *Zodiac*, by David Fincher, released in 2007. This is a good enough movie. I have a ridiculous wealth of knowledge about the Zodiac Killer, as, like most pot-smoking 'artists' in their early twenties, I spent a lot of time engrossed in conspiracy theories. (I just now erased three paragraphs where I couldn't help but inform you of the lady in the polka dot dress, MK Ultra, Sirhan Sirhan, etc.) Essentially though, *Zodiac*, six years after the World Trade Center came down, served to provide a new, and also old, conspiracy for Americans to spend two hours with. To get them out of the real conspiracy brewing around 'jet fuel can't melt steel beams' and 'it was an inside job.' The irony here is that those who know of the Zodiac case know that it goes deep into the heart of the filthy American Military Industrial Complex. (I just now erased that Jim Jones was a CIA agent conducting an experiment in mass mind control, and I erased that most of the Symbionese Liberation Army, kidnappers of Patty Hearst, were mostly all CIA agents working under the black and turned once clockwise umbrella of COINTELPRO).

The Zodiac Killer bombed a plane in order to kill one person. The Zodiac Killer was cleaning up certain people connected to Operation Magnolia, otherwise known as MK Ultra. (I can't stop myself from reminding people that the male victim of the very first Zodiac shooting, referred to only briefly in the film, was wearing many sweaters and pants in the heat of a California summer, because she had to die and he knew it was coming). The Fincher film uses a case that has fascinated people for decades, a deep and unsolvable mystery, to refocus the American public's attention for a few hours; to draw them away from the living conspiracy that led to women and children being killed in Iraq and Afghanistan. Fincher (Hollywood) used a film which would not exist without a malevolent American intelligence apparatus to distract people from their daily lives which are affected by a malevolent American intelligence apparatus.

Ferris Bueller's Day Off was a shorter review, mostly focused on Reaganomics with a brief entrée into cold war issues. Primarily in my review of *Bueller*, I discussed the skill of the wardrobe department in accurately portraying the style of the time.

Last week, I attempted a retroactive review of *Weekend at Bernie's* but gave up and realized that in the end, cocaine in the 1980's caused a great many movies to be green-lighted that would never see the light of day now.

4.

In my paintings, I work with what people call 'genres.' Still life, landscape, figuration. I don't paint them in the way you might imagine. I subvert genres. I like to make serious things seem light; light things seem serious. This is also important in comedy. I like comedy, it's the most exalted art form.I think I'm a funny person and people have confirmed it for me. In fact, I recently wrote my first joke of 2016, and it's surprisingly family-friendly. It goes like this:

> What did the winter coat say to the old lady?
> Don't say I never warmed you.

It's not a bad joke. Nobody gets offended, and children can appreciate it too if they know the phrase 'Don't say I never warned you'. I like genres and I like to manipulate them. I enjoy disappointing and surprising, at the same time if possible. (I don't, however, want people to be surprised that they're disappointed with my work; disappointed that they like my work is ideal).

I'm also drawn to themes. The big ones: death, sex. Others too. Themes and genres provide the audience with a sense of comfort, and if you throw in a traditional narrative, you can't disappoint. Being able to cause discomfort using forms and structures people are ordinarily comforted by interests me. This mirrors my early life, in that I was born into a typical narrative with all the themes and structures present, but they were always askew, out of focus, interrupted and false. This caused me great discomfort. I suppose I have a desire then to pass that feeling on. Not to be cruel, but to connect with others whose narratives were fractured too.

5.

My brother Leslie was a drug addict out on the west coast. Occasionally I'd call one of the guys he was close to, ask if he was okay. They'd ask if I wanted him to come to the phone, but once I knew he was alive enough to come to the phone I'd hang up. I had nothing to say to him. I loved him. He was my brother. But I knew from my own life that I couldn't help him. And unless he was helped, or helped himself, he was a nightmare. My mother wrote him off a long time ago, and she was justified in doing so. I was his emergency contact. He didn't ask if this was okay, I would just find out whenever the area code for Vancouver showed up on my phone: ambulance, police, detox, hospital. For Leslie I existed as a number signifying an attachment to a world he'd shuttered out. There was something beautiful in that, in the simplicity of what I had become to my brother.

A cliché about family. No matter what, you always love them.

6.

Recently, I finished a long essay ahead of deadline. After that, movies. I have always been drawn to two cliché scenes in film. One is the person walking down a street, usually in New York or Paris, in the rain, crying. Either unrestrainedly or subtly, tears lost in sheets of rain. Something about it, each time I see it, I feel a sense of home.

The other scene I like is more complex and typically seen on crime shows: a cop, bad news and a couple in their home. Daughter was missing; daughter was found dead. It can be any type of death. The couple is at home, either clueless as to what the knock on the door is about to do to them, or unkempt and unslept, waiting on word of what has happened to their loved one. A cop (they will typically in a preceding scene talk about how this is the worst part of the job. *Notifying the family.*) parks his car on the street and gets out. The married couple is either watching television, arguing, or sitting at the kitchen table, sullen and puffy-eyed. The cop approaches the door and knocks. The couple asks him inside. The cop asks the couple to sit down. If they already know something is wrong, they will refuse to sit down. Whether the couple is sitting or standing, the notifying officer breaks the bad news. Your son was killed in an avalanche. Yes, we found your daughter; no she's, no I'm sorry. This type of language. Then, and I love it each time I see it, the mother will attack the cop. She unleashes all the shock and disbelief and horrible sadness she feels in that instant onto this bastard who has come to tell her bad news. She flails at the cop and punches his chest over and over. Sometimes she swears at him and calls him a liar. He does nothing to defend himself. This can go on for as little as a few seconds or up to a minute, depending on the director. Then at a certain point the husband (somehow always immune to shock and full of stoic resolve) will pull his wife off the officer and she'll bury her face in his chest. The officer will slowly back out of the house, uttering a bleak apology. Together the couple will cry, a union of stunned grief.

7.

I've always wanted to make art and not consider how it might be received, not think of it as a commodity. To just let my instincts drag me down some irrational path and see what happens. So I posted on Facebook that I needed three actors for a short video—"I can't offer any compensation except to be included in my dubious body of work"—then a day later I had three.

I picked a husband and wife because I figured if they weren't actors, there might at least be some natural chemistry between them. They were in their late thirties and rather average-looking. I mean their clothing was average-looking. This wouldn't work for me with hipsters. Hipsters aren't visited by unseen tragedy (unless the mother kombucha falls off a ledge and breaks) and they'd also cause the video to look dated in the future. So Colin and Jamie it was. They'd been married four years. For a moment, I imagined them thinking this might be something that could be 'fun for their marriage' and I became terribly sad. The detective was to be played by a guy in his early thirties, Desmond, who owned a grey suit and didn't have a beard. He looked like he could pull it off. All of this was to be shot from inside my apartment through a window and across the street anyway, so they'd all be rather small characters in the background of a larger scene.

8.

I hadn't felt this excited about anything in a while. I told my wife Cristine all about it on Skype. She liked the idea very much. She'd be home from the UK in a month and I was looking forward to showing her.

The neighbors across the street and I were friendly, so I asked them if they'd let me use their porch and front door for a video I wanted to make. I promised I'd make them lasagna if they gave me ten minutes of access. They said yes, and Brad, you don't need to make us lasagna (which, thank God because I've never made lasagna and it seems incredibly complex).

I took Colin and Jamie to lunch the day beforehand to give them a brief description of what I wanted. They were excited. Too excited. I felt a bit sad again. I met Desmond later that evening, standing outside an art opening. I hid in a doorway until he came out to meet me. He was enthusiastic too. His role was simpler: look like a cop, act like a cop and be ready to be hit in the chest. He smiled and said no problem. I was jealous of what a great set of teeth he had.

9.

The day of the 'shoot'—I cringed typing that. The day of the recording? The day of the shoot, I woke up and I did the same thing I do every day. I drank a large Vega chocolate smoothie and watched NBC and CBC news from the night before. I took seven medications. I had a thirty-minute nap then got ready. Around one, I peeked through my front window and saw all three of the 'players' approaching my house. I watched Desmond and the married couple introduce themselves. Desmond really looked like a cop. This made me wonder about him as a person for a moment. I went outside to go over it all again, then took them across the street to meet the neighbors, who both seemed hungover and were cradling each other in a hammock on their porch. I ran everyone through the routine yet again. They all assured me they understood, so I returned to my apartment.

I set my camera on the ledge of my window, zoomed in on the area in front of my neighbor's house, pressed record, then texted Desmond to begin walking. I really did feel excited. All of this was new to me. Painting and writing were brutal isolation; this was interactive, and the most social thing I'd done in a long time. I looked at the screen of my camera. There Desmond came from the left, walking stoically towards the house. He was far enough away, and my camera poor enough, that his features weren't too clear. This worked. I loved the grey suit. He looked like the cliché of a wearied cop. As Desmond approached the front of the house and walked up the stairs I moved the camera to follow him. He knocked at the door. After ten or twelve seconds the front door opened. Colin answered it and Jamie stood behind him. Desmond displayed his passport which was meant to be a police badge, and Jamie stepped out from behind Colin. Desmond stepped back. All three of them were on the porch now. I was surprised and then delighted that I could hear Jamie scream 'LIAR!'—how did she know I'd want that? Then

I saw Colin try to put his arm in front of Jamie but he was too late. I watched her punch Desmond dead center in his chest. He stumbled back a step and stayed there. Jamie was really sobbing now, pulling at her shirt and clawing at Desmond while Colin got behind her and tried to keep her still. Colin got a good hold of Jamie, and I could hear her screaming unintelligibly at Desmond. Then like a ballerina, Jamie, held by Colin from behind, spun herself around and buried herself in his chest. Desmond stood totally still, returning his passport to his jacket, and then—I could see this part clearly—Colin backed slowly inside with Jamie then shut the door, all while maintaining eye contact with Desmond. Desmond did this great thing where he lowered his head as if to say this is the worst part of the job, notifying the family, then turned around and began to walk down the stairs.

I kept my camera fixed on the front of the door of the house while Desmond exited the frame to the left. God, it was great. Exactly how I'd envisioned it and even better. Jamie killed it. What a great scream. I was electrified. I texted them a minute later and they all came to my front door, their faces excited and full of words.

I took them for lunch up the street at Duffy's.

10.

The first time Cristine and I met, I thought her eyes looked like bowls of radium. Something about being apart from your partner for a while, you're shocked at how good-looking they are when they return. If not that, the love you feel for them. Unless you're in that other situation. That's a bad situation.

Cristine had come home three days before, and after helping her unpack, after _____ and the rest, I wanted to show her the video I made. She said I sounded like a little kid. I was excited. I'm rarely excited. She was anxious to see, and honestly I wanted to see it yet another time. Watching it with someone else was like watching a movie; it felt like I hadn't made it. She told me it was good, and my satisfaction was complete. She asked me what I wanted to do with it. I said I didn't want to do anything with it. I did it to do it. To own it. To recapture and contain on my hard drive for eternity a moment from culture that touched me, and that I'd recreated to look at whenever I want.

It was so nice having her home.

11.

We spent the next two weeks buying things for the house. Dish racks and cutting boards and hanging racks for clothes. One day we were heading out to High Park, and as we shut the front door behind us, I saw a man in a cheap suit and worn shoes making his way into our yard. He looked at me and continued up the stairs to the landing without saying anything.

'Are you Brad Phillips?' he said.

Cristine stood slightly behind me. I came down two steps and the three of us stood there, a bit too close to each other.

'Can I help you with something?' I asked.

I knew from my own time alive that real tragedy doesn't employ the telephone. It requires a human being. He reached his left hand into the right inside pocket of his jacket. I knew Leslie had died before this man had time to produce his police badge. I saw it all unfold the way I saw it in movies, the way I saw it in the video I'd made. He said he was sorry but Leslie had overdosed and this time he hadn't made it. Cristine clenched my arm tightly. In my head I saw all the images from the all the films that had comforted me. I saw the thrashing, the screaming, the disbelief. Then I heard my mouth say, 'Thank you for letting me know.'

The officer seemed confused by my lack of response. I was confused by my lack of response too. I loved Leslie. He was family, but I felt nothing. I felt this ostensibly bad news come towards me, enter through the hole in my psyche, or soul, and exit out the back of my consciousness. The hole trauma had built in me was so large that Andrew's death couldn't fill it. It couldn't even touch it. It was like a successful jump shot that didn't hit the rim and hardly grazed the net. I watched the news of Andrew's death bounce away from me. I heard the police officer providing me with details, but I wasn't really listening. I was thinking about how good Cristine smelled earlier in the bed, and how we'd better get to the park before it was too crowded.

The cop walked away. Cristine asked if I was really okay and I said I really was.

Thirty minutes later I was showing her how to get chipmunks to eat peanuts right out of her hand and we were both laughing.

12.

It's two months later and it's the beginning of winter. Yesterday Cristine and I got off the subway and I stopped at the corner store like I always did for Gatorade, Nag Champa and cigarettes. Cristines head was wrapped in a scarf and her nose was running. I had my jacket open and was glad it wasn't summer anymore. We left the store and crossed the street. As we got closer to our house, I noticed an older white woman in a grey pantsuit and open black wool jacket lingering ahead of us. We kept walking towards home. The woman stopped in front of our house. I felt my whole body begin to sweat and pulled my jacket shut. Cristine didn't notice anything.

I said, 'Look at that woman. She looks like a cop, no?'

Cristine said, 'It's hard to tell. She just looks cold.'

'Why is she standing there?' I asked.

My wife said nothing.

A few feet from the walkway to our place, the woman made eye contact with me. I saw her mouth open as if in slow motion, her lips grotesque caterpillars. My insides felt how the sky looks when a tornado is coming. I squeezed Cristine's hand, which was in my pocket for warmth, and she asked what was wrong. I couldn't speak. Everything was happening so slowly. The woman was about to speak when suddenly I started sobbing uncontrollably. Cristine and the woman both looked at me. I heard myself scream 'Get out of here!' and Cristine looked at me, confused. The woman looked scared. I couldn't stop crying. Hiccough crying, kid crying. My mustache was damp and cold crusted from my leaking nose. I heard it again. 'Go away!' It was me but it wasn't me. I crumpled against the snow-heavy shrub in front of my house, bawling. The woman backed up a few steps and Cristine approached her.

'Is there something wrong?' she asked the cop.

'I was wondering if you had the time,' I heard the cop reply.

She just wanted to know the time. She wasn't a cop, she was a woman who didn't know what time it was. My crying slowed down. Cristine pulled her phone out of her pocket. 'It's eleven forty-five,' she said. But the woman looked even more confused. Cristine's phone was still set to U.K. time.

NOTHING PERSONAL

It's rare that I give lectures or talks, primarily because I'm not asked to. However, six months ago I was contacted by a 'sexologist' from Brussels who was coordinating a symposium on atypical sexuality where all the speakers were artists or writers, not doctors or scientists. I asked what he wanted me to speak about. He said that based on my work and 'public profile,' he'd like me to discuss something having to do with surveillance in contemporary culture; the possibility of controlling one's public image; whether or not artists have an obligation to mutual consent when documenting the lives of others; is privacy dead, do I care if it's dead; do I take pleasure in watching or being watched, listening or being listened to, recording or being recorded, being followed or following others; are there ways that I can cope with these things—all of this under the umbrella of sex and sexuality. I came up with something I remember sounding much like this, my voice projecting these words from a dais to an audience of apparent mutes. I believe it to be culled from my personal life. I believe it may be true. I think it's possible it really is.

BEFORE I BEGIN, I'D LIKE TO ADD MY BRIEF REACTION to the insightful lecture, which was a privilege to have been present for, that I now must follow. First, let's address the elephant in the room. You know, I used to buy jib—what would you call it here?—crystal methamphetamine, from a guy named Mikey Foucault. Having never read a book before, other than *The Turner Diaries*, he had no idea he shared his name with a prominent figure. So, Dr. Julia Kristeva, esteemed scholar from Waco, Texas, I salute you for not changing your name, forging ahead as Dr. Kristeva. In doing so you've set a high bar for yourself, and I think that's worth applauding.

What interested me about Dr. Kristeva's lecture was her analysis of fetishes and their origins. While we all agree that many fetishes most certainly find their genesis in a moment from childhood where a sexual feeling collided with an inanimate object, there remain those fetishes, *paraphilias*, for which there is no childhood source. I myself have wondered whether sadomasochism can sometimes be a fetish (which sadly, in a long list of paraphilias, is the only one classified as a mental illness) which is not triggered by pre-pubescent experiences. I can say, as someone who's had sadomasochistic impulses ever since I was a small child, that some of us can find no moment from our childhoods which explain our needs. My conclusion is that some people are born with specific sexual needs; that atypical sexuality can at times be genetic, not sourced in infancy.

So, following Dr. Kristeva's research into the lives of couples with unusual sex lives, I want to mention that I feel not enough work has gone into examining the significant danger of emotional and sexual dissatisfaction which can arise when one partner is not able to indulge their particular fetish within the confines of a loving relationship. One friend I spoke with compared the time he spent repressing his masochistic impulses to what homosexual friends have described as the lonely pain of unrealized selfhood experienced while in the closet. I think there must be further discussion about the needless suffering and sublimated frustration that can often infect otherwise happy, loving relationships, when one partner is not permitted to be their true sexual self. What suffering is in store for the masochist whose wife will not punish him? What suffering awaits the sadist who cannot bend her husband over her knee?

Some people will disagree. They will say that the masochist or voyeur was not 'born that way.' But can we say with absolute certainty that for some people this was not precisely the case? I am certain that at least some people here today can find no locatable trigger for their needs; that instead they feel their atypical sexual desires to be as much a part of their DNA as the color of their eyes. Until more research is devoted to this subject, relationships that might otherwise thrive and be full of love will continue to suffer and disintegrate; and people will needlessly repress what might otherwise be healthily explored. So, thank you Dr. Kristeva for helping me further contextualize some of the ideas I've been mulling over for quite some time.

Now, on to the topic I was asked to speak about. Thank you for your indulgence.

I was asked to speak about how I cope with various things regarding privacy, publicity, self-image, much more. I can cope with anything. I cope in ways that hurt myself and hurt others, that help myself and help others. I cope obliquely, neurotically, ritualistically and boringly. I practically cope professionally. I'm a coper. To be close to me is also to learn how to cope—to cope with how I cope. Cope the way you cope with a punch in the stomach, your car hitting a tree, all your bones breaking spontaneously. I am a small island of coping, and those who wash up on my island are introduced to coping in ways that they never imagined. Cope with me. Cope-dependent.

Am I experimenting? Yes. Do I take pleasure in watching, listening, recording and following; being watched, listened to, recorded and followed? Yes. Is it possible to control our public image? Yes. My entire body of work is an effort to control my public image by way of a comprehensive disguise. I work very hard at crafting an idea of myself to be consumed when I die. My work is all meant to be viewed properly once I die, and it's all fake and it's all real and it's all my own doing. Do we have any obligations? No. Is privacy dead and do I care? No and No.

All of my work, painting and writing and photography, is in some way about the manipulation of my image. I am sincerely crafting, over the course of my life, a suicide note in fiction, essays, paintings and photographs.

Novels, suicide notes and memoirs all have one thing in common: they're all fictions. Novels, obviously. Memoirs, while promising the truth of a life, are still inherently fictional by virtue of what's excluded and what's amplified. Memoirs are the manipulative presentation of one's life for public consumption. The mundane and the embarrassing are usually left out. Suicide notes are fiction in that they appeal to the reader with urgent desperation to believe something. Believe in the effort the depressed person made to stay alive. Believe in their sense of worthlessness. Believe that whomever they blame for their mental and emotional calamities truly is to blame. The suicide note writer is selling the reader the truth of their suffering. They're trying to tell the reader that their death is legitimate, necessary. Suicides notes are fictions crafted to impart the authenticity of the writers suffering and subsequent death. They are fictions too in that they give one-sided narratives to something endlessly complex.

I recently had to write a bio for an art exhibition. It said, 'Brad Philips is an artist and writer, born in 1973 who lives and works in Kingston, Jamaica.'

I was born in 1974 and live in Scarborough, Canada.

I've become so good at manipulating my public image that many people now believe I truly do live in Jamaica, or last year Lithuania, and that I am a little older than I am, or, a few years ago, a little younger. All my work is an attempt to spread disinformation about myself, so that nobody actually knows who I am, but everyone thinks they know a great deal about me.

I'll begin with my partner and myself, Lazara for the remainder of this lecture. For the next year and change we'll be living a continent apart. We met while she was living in China. We were both in failing relationships. We met via Instagram. We are a voyeur and an exhibitionist, and a voyeur/exhibitionist.

On Instagram, Lazara was posting images of mistranslated shirts she saw in China. 'Slut' emblazoned on the tiny shirt of an infant; other sad jokes like that, often poignant or poetic. Women contacted me on Instagram often back then for sexual reasons. I was unable to grasp why it kept occurring. Lazara pointed out that it was likely due to the nature of what I was posting, which were (the account has since been deleted) private BDSM photos and similar images culled from online. Obscure fetishes, frightened faces, my own large hands, plastic panties. I have a new account and it persists, perhaps because I also publish writing about sex and make artwork about sex. It's become tiresome.

As a man, I'm aware that to go through a woman's account and like every photograph of her is the equivalent of honking at her from a car at a stoplight. It's painfully obvious, and I prefer to be intentionally ambiguous. Serendipitously, one day I found Lazara's account. I liked all her photos of shirts, because I truly did like them, but purposefully did not like photos of her face or body, which I also liked very much. She looked at my page, saw we shared common interests, and sent me a message. I sent one back. Her public display of her private interests allowed me access to her private mind, and later to her private body.

While she was in China she lived with her then-boyfriend. My ex-girlfriend had happily moved far away, and was swaddled in bitterness. Lazara would Skype with me when she had time alone. There were also times when she'd Skype with me while her boyfriend was there. Due to certain predilections of mine, I liked it a great deal when she would be talking to me, often sexually, and type that her boyfriend had walked into the room, then turn off her microphone. I enjoyed the way she would cast quick bored glances at me waiting for him to leave. I got off on her showing me her small breasts, or telling me how much she wanted to see me seconds before and after her boyfriend's shadow appeared on the wall behind her.

I am not a good person. I'm also not a bad person. These dualities don't really register with me in the first place. I only believe in intentions. My intentions were never to shame her boyfriend. Or his shame was a happy byproduct of our situation. We were both desperately lonely and unable to express our true natures in the context of a loving relationship.

I am also not a good person.

While Lazara was in China I was inadvisably alone. It was the first time in my life when I wasn't living with a woman. I was, however, engaged in a specific sexual relationship with another young woman, Nicole (privacy), who had also contacted me via Instagram. The relationship I had with this girl was healthy. We both wanted nothing outside of the sexual services we provided for each other.

Nicole was a lesbian. Nicole hated men. Nicole was a submissive who couldn't accept that she was a submissive. She dominated girls but secretly needed to be dominated by a man when she could get it.

We started communicating before I met Lazara. We decided to meet after a few weeks at a diner, where I immediately felt total sexual satisfaction observing her nervousness. Nicole and I then began to participate in sometimes brutal but mostly standard BDSM type activity. Once, I kept her 'captive' in my basement suite for a week, in part for sexual reasons, but also because my landlady who lived upstairs was fucking Nicole's mother's ex-boyfriend, so she couldn't be seen with me.

She also just couldn't be seen with me. She looked like my daughter, and behaved with me publicly the way no daughter should with her dad.

I let Nicole sit in my bed and do her work dominating bald, grey, pitiful men on Femdom websites. I liked watching her do it. She would message me privately from the bed while I watched from the couch, asking if there was any specific way I wanted her to humiliate the men, and because I loathe men, there were things I had her do for me. Occasionally she incorporated me in her work, but never my face. I'd use my hands to lift her shirt to the bottom of her breasts, and listen to the men whimper and throw money at her, then lower her shirt again. The men called me Sir. They never saw me. I was a disembodied hand putting ice cream in Nicole's mouth from out of frame while she told them how pathetic they were. They would comment on her pretty lips, whining that they wanted them on their cocks, and then my hand would enter their field of vision, grab her by the hair and make her disappear, only to pop up later with red cheeks, wiping her mouth. She would smile at me out of frame.

These men were suffering terribly, which I enjoyed, but after a while she didn't, because what they wanted was to suffer, and she was giving them just that. I, however, did not stop enjoying dominating these men by proxy through my young friend who I myself dominated.

Nicole was involved in financial domination too and would send the men screenshots of themselves manipulating their sad beige dicks and threaten to show them to their wives and children unless they gave her money. And like dumb addicts they gave her that money. I would then use that money to buy her ice-cream, which she loved, and reward her with it if she could endure what I put her through.

I admired that this twenty-year-old girl had so much power over these men, who were often wealthy 50-something-year-old executives, because I knew that when I had her, I could turn her into a puddle on my floor with just two fingers or a certain expression. I enjoyed the contrast. Together Nicole and I were manipulating private and public. I was always hidden, she was often exposed. The men were always exposed.

I also witnessed the way money moves in the space between private and public.

Lazara was interested in my sexual life. Each thing I thought would repulse her instead drew her closer to me. Everything I felt certain she would judge me harshly for she accepted with curiosity. Or something beyond curiosity.

At the time I was also untangling myself from another long-distance situation, which was entirely about power and control. Lazara was interested in the ways I was able to manipulate the behavior of this woman, who I'll call Nisanur, simply through what I wrote her and how I wrote it. Nisanur explained she wanted my permission to sleep, go to the bathroom; all of it initiated by her once I made it clear she could ask that from me. She couldn't get dressed for work until I picked one of three items I'd told her to offer me as options. I decided whether she would wear underwear to work, she'd thank me, and I'd go on with the rest of my day.

Nisanur was an extremely masochistic woman. The exercises I had her endure for me would always be rewarded with kindness, and eventual assistance in helping her achieve orgasm before I'd give her a few hours to herself. Hours she preferred that I would own. She once told me to push her past 'every limit and fear and neurosis I have. I want you to break me down to my most basic parts, then teach me how to rebuild myself properly.' I'd heard the submissive men Nicole dominated say similar things.

Nisanur had contacted me first. Soon we were excited to have found each other. The attraction between us was intense and soon very intimate. She told me how badly she was being deprived of her sexual needs by a husband that thought they were unnatural. It became clear early on that I could adeptly provide them to her, and with dedication.

Nisanur was a germaphobe, something we wanted to confront sexually. I've found in relationships like this, there's an impulse on both the part of the sadist and the masochist to find the weak spot, then work away at it until it becomes a sweet spot. Any sadist will attest to the immense sense of pride and satisfaction masochists display when they're able to endure things that they felt at first unable to endure. After dark moments in scary places, you'll often be treated to an almost innocent smile of proud accomplishment.

Lazara was sexually dissatisfied in China, and curious for reasons of her own about the sexuality I was involved in. I'm still involved in this kind of sexuality—sexuality that's always been so much of who I am that I feel like it's been in me since birth. What seemed to amaze Lazara most was how I exercised this fact of my nature with a woman who lived in a different city than me; that my domination of a happily subservient masochist transpired exclusively in a non-physical space, and was as satisfying as anything done in person.

I sent Lazara documentation and details. Photos and videos of Nicole interacting very intensely with my body, one Lazara had never touched. I told her stories about Nisanur; how she squirmed and endured on video in her bathroom for me, her lithe and muscular body covered with clothespins in spots where the body least wants them: bruised knees on a hard tile floor for an hour, practicing saying "Thank you" quietly to the camera with her arms behind her back and something vibrating inside of her. Nicole let me send images of her to Lazara because she knew I had feelings for her. Nisanur, who I was slowly disentangling myself from, didn't know anyone else was aware of her, but the nature of our agreement made that none of her business. She had literally, in a witnessed contract, agreed to be in this position and enjoyed it. Stories alone were arousing to Lazara, and throughout my time with her, no one ever saw what Nisanur looked like. Symbolism is a heavy thing in this world. Just through knowing she had consented to my disseminating pornographic images of her, essentially handing me her life in the form of JPEG's, Nisanur found herself in a near-constant state of arousal. While I would have never acted on my threats I was convincing, because she needed to believe I'd do what I'd said— the threat is the lubricant. I also needed her to be convincing for me, and she was. Now she'll remain in her locked private folder, on my hard drive for me to enjoy until I'm dead. Something she'd like, forever encaged in a technologic cell.

Like the men Nicole made money from, Nisanur also got off on a sort of financial domination, more akin to life explosion domination. She liked it most when I sent her screenshots of herself naked on her hands and knees in the bathroom, her body sprouting strange insertions, putatively about to be sent to her husband, or mother or sister if she disobeyed any of my capricious rules. She wanted to engage in a fantasized lack of consent. Nisanur's primarily sexual arousal was generated by her relinquishing control in our relationship - unless she said one agreed upon word, and the simulation would end immediately. The closer I got to blowing her life up, the more turned on she became. I had the passwords to her email account and her bank account. I had a key to where she worked in Chicago. I had everything of hers that people consider private, all of it given to me freely in pursuit of her own arousal. Before it was given, she'd begged for it to be taken from her. She consented to having her privacy shattered if she misbehaved or misspoke. My having so much power over her private life, her relinquishing consent to me, was very sexual for her.

Obviously, it was also very sexual for me.

When I once showed Nisanur a screenshot of me adding her mother as a friend on Facebook, she said it was like 'the sky ripping a hole' through her pussy. The state of privacy in contemporary society is of no interest to me. I benefit from the complexities of manipulating the lives of others. With different agreements about what privacy meant to each woman, everything I did—with Lazara, Nicole, Nisanur—was documented and recorded obsessively. I was in Chicago in April of last year, and I didn't see Nisanur, but I photographed myself near her work and near her home. When I got back to Canada, I sent her those photographs, and she pleaded with me to see her, assuming I was there. I used my documentation of my time in Chicago to fuck with her—her sexual needs, her sense of ease. To turn her on and to make her believe this might be the day she'd walk out of work and find me waiting for her. Important and hard for some people to believe is that this is exactly what she wanted. She was a woman whose g-spot was inside her amygdala. This surfeit of surveillance and documentation, confusion of public and private, gave me a lot of satisfaction; it also satisfied her, and by learning about what I did and was doing with my life before we met, satisfied Lazara as well.

I should add that telling Nicole what I was putting Nisanur through daily was the clincher in having her meet me, and led to the subsequent sexual trials I put her through. Submissive people are always turned on by seeing that you're able to dominate others, so in this regard my documentation of one sexual experience allowed me to access another sexual experience, which I then used to contribute to yet a third sexual experience, with Lazara.

I was spending time with Nicole whenever she could break free from her much older sugar daddy. Having only shown Lazara images and video of what happened with Nicole after it was over, she asked if I would let her watch me and Nicole on Skype.

I never imagined I'd find a woman who would ask this of me.

I liked that she did, and to this day still sometimes thinks of perverse things that don't occur to me. This wasn't something I'd ever done or considered before, but the situation was aligned so that it suddenly became a perfect way for us to connect sexually from opposite corners of the world.

As I've said, Nicole is a lesbian who's dominant with women, so when I told her she was going to do this with me, she wasn't very pleased about it. However, the dynamic that existed between us made it quite easy to change her mind. The part of her that dominated women took hold of the idea that someone who wanted to fuck me but couldn't would be watching us and would most likely feel frustrated. If Nicole got pleasure out of that scenario it was of her own imagining, because Lazara is a genuine voyeur who also enjoys deprivation. She only wanted to watch, not even masturbate. It was her presence on a blank screen on my laptop, no voice, no face—that was precisely what aroused her.

So I booked a hotel room for me and Nicole because I didn't want to worry about noise and visibility. China is twelve hours ahead of here, so I had Nicole meet me around dinner time. We fooled around in the hotel a bit, went and bought food (her being much smaller than me, and being so servile, she found a lot of pleasure in carrying the heavy grocery basket around the store for me. She once had an orgasm tying my shoelace in public), we came back and watched television until it was nine o' clock, which is when Lazara told me she'd be waking up and available.

I put my laptop on a desk in the hotel room then called Lazara on Skype. I wrote that she should turn off her microphone and camera and she did. I wrote that I wished it was her instead of Nicole. I did wish that. Nicole was grumpy about what was happening. I helped her get over that quickly with my left hand. Eventually she forgot about the fact that someone else was watching us, and we did what we often did then, which involved restraint and pain, orgasms and sex. Various noises which would confuse anyone in the next room. While I was doing what I was doing, I didn't forget that Lazara, who at this point I had serious feelings for, was watching early in the morning from a squalid room in China.

Maybe this has been too dark for some of you. I could have told other stories, stories about 'regular sex.' I did consciously leave out some brutal color and detail. But these have been my premiere experiences with surveillance, privacy, consent and documentation. In any case, this is sexology. I can't imagine anyone is doing further research in dimly lit, missionary position sex. Not unless sex reaches some nadir where dimly lit, missionary position sex becomes the new perverse.

Rush ahead, fast forward, plummet into the abyss of the recent past. Old fashioned experiences of the modern scenarios described above. I am in London with Lazara. It is spring in Europe. I am happy to be with the woman I love. We finally get some sexual and emotional relief. Nicole is gone. My ex is a happily forgotten memory. Nisanur is gone. Lazara's ex is gone. We are no longer hiding or lying. We are weightless and new.

I think we have an interesting sex life. That we spent our first two visits together in neutral cities where neither of us had connections allowed us to be more experimental, to bring home strangers, to embrace our antisocial instincts. It's possible we're horrible perverts. You wouldn't know it to look at us, and that's what's beautiful about sexual specialists. We hide in plain sight.

In the Highgate section of London is a club called Rio's. A relaxation spa. A sex club. Everything about it is perfect, anachronistic, frozen in time in the pre-AIDS, post-pill sexual utopia of the great swingers era. Lazara had been wanting to take me for a while. It's a place where you must be naked, where you must be exposed; where there is very little privacy, and that privacy can be transacted and elasticized. Lazara has a sexually and physically perfect body. Swingers, and I say this without prejudice, tend to be overweight and generally unattractive people, usually in their fifties or sixties. In this club, Lazara's unimaginable body stands out like pornography. I don't care about tattoos, but I happen to have a body covered by them entirely. So together we are in Rio's rather noticeable. Men ogle, respectfully enough, and in any case this is a place where ogling is not impolite. It's expected, accepted.

We sit in a steam room. Men stroke their cocks and stare at her. I get complimented about my tattoos, but I am not the focus. If any attention is given to me, it's by men who give me approving looks about the beauty of my girlfriend. As we walk around the circuit of steam rooms, saunas and pools, the same half dozen men follow us. They attempt to be discreet like undercover cops, but in reality, like undercover cops, they are extremely obvious. We sit in a steam room together. Lazara has perfect posture, high breasts, a flat stomach, Bernini-sculpted ribs. A Persian man strokes his cock, staring at her body. He looks at me obligingly. I like this. She likes this. It's too hot for me. Eventually Lazara wants to take me into the one of the private rooms.

As we go inside I see the same coterie of men tailing us. As I close the door suddenly three or four men ask if they can come in and watch us. I look at Lazara, she shakes her head, I tell them no and shut them out. Inside, the decor is ideal. Two mats, a garbage can, everything wood. I lay on my back and Lazara gives me head. I can hear clambering outside. Sounds of arguing. I hear a woman tell a man that if the room is occupied he can't linger and to keep on walking. I hear more arguing. Lazara gets on top of me. The contrast is appealing. We're in a locked box of a room built to fuck in, and outside there is only tension. I know this tension is being generated by those same half dozen men, including the ones who wanted to watch us. I know they're hanging around just outside the room.

In that room, we are completely private. But I can hear the greedy public, wanting to see my girlfriend get fucked; to see her wet body moving on wet plastic. The rooms are all made of wood, but the walls are thin. I can hear almost everything from outside the room, and assume they can hear the sounds from inside. Lazara wants to come and asks me if she can. She is not quiet. I say yes. She has an orgasm. She says thank you three times. She is not quiet.I know the men outside can hear her. I don't have an orgasm myself, but I get a great deal of pleasure from knowing there's a group of very frustrated males lingering outside our room. It satisfies me in many ways. We lay there for a bit and decide to leave.

When I open the heavy door I see I wasn't wrong, and the same half dozen guys are sitting on benches near us. They're all polite and quiet now. I watch as they stare with anguished yearning at my future wife's recently-fucked, post-orgasmic body. We walk back to the change rooms and they tail off.

Outside the club we step back into 2015. We share a cigarette and wait for our car to come, and on the ride home Lazara rests her head on my shoulder. I open the window and cool down with the help of breezy modern European air, as our car drives past dozens of CCTV cameras that have no idea what we've just done.

MOM AND DAD, DELETED SCENES

My therapist tells me it's important to write. I'm supposed to be doing this to "process" my feelings. The following is what "Andrew," who prefers I not call him Dr. Babcock (causing me to take him far less seriously), suggested I write when I told him I often spent time wondering what my parents would have been like if they'd never had children. I admit to being shocked at what came out. The more I've read it though—having spent twenty-two of my forty-three years knowing my father rather intimately—the more it seems sort of reasonable, not quite as science-fictive as it did the day I finished it. I remembered just now that the only piece of advice my father ever gave me was that you can beat a lie detector test by clenching your asshole before each question.

T HE YEAR IS 1981. BERNIE AND SOPHIA HAVE BEEN married since 1972. Nine happy years. Bernie is handsome in a sort of low-level criminal way. Two gold chains, one with a star of David on the end, although he isn't Jewish. One gold bracelet and many chunky rings typical of the era. He has a not quite mountain-man but not closely cropped beard, almost black save a silver-dollar sized patch of white on the left side of his chin. He's five foot six but usually wears cowboy boots, often at home, so always seems taller. His eyes are that rare and sometimes spooky light sky blue usually associated with psychopaths. On the inside of his left forearm is a tattoo of a cartoon devil face. It's worn and blown out, like he either got it in highschool, or in prison. Bernie was fired from his job eight months ago, and Sophia doesn't know this. Bernie has family money, so there aren't the typical economic peculiarities to alert Sophia that something isn't quite right.

Sophia is a grade school teacher. She teaches mathematics and, twice a week, physical education. Grades three and four. Sophia is neither beautiful nor unattractive. Her high cheekbones and deep green eyes lead people to call her 'striking.' She is slightly taller than her husband and extremely thin. Her dirty blonde hair ends at the middle of her bum. She often keeps it in two long braids for a week straight before untying them to wash, after which she'll braid again. Without the braids her hair is too free, getting in her mouth, getting caught on things. She typically wears bell-bottom jeans and those mesh football jerseys that don't advertise any particular team, over which she'll wear either a shawl or a loosely knit wool cardigan.

They are thirty-five and thirty-three respectively.

When Sophia met Bernie he was a heroin addict. But not a gimpy, unshaven, disease-ridden heroin addict. A heroin addict with a manageable habit. Sophia, being fond of the occasional line of cocaine, was not one to judge. They told each other as the wedding got nearer that they'd each clean up. They wanted to have a family. This was before they found out that that Bernie was sterile, and the waiting list to adopt was so long that they'd not have a child until they were of such an age that said child would become odd and easily bullied. This was Bernie's opinion anyway, having been born when his mother was forty-three. He told Sophia that kids like him stood out, having taken on the references and idiosyncrasies of their too-old parents. So they decided against children and instead opted for a cottage. A place on a lake, near a stream, by a pond, in the woods; a place to get away from their troubles. That they had no real troubles didn't mean to Bernie and Sophia that they should be excluded from this classic North American dream.

Sophia quit cocaine quite easily, as is possible with cocaine, unless you start using crack, which was not much on the scene by the time she put the last line to bed. Later Sophia would often remark that crack had given cocaine a bad name. Bernie however was struggling to curtail his heroin use. Heroin is not easily curtailed. Heroin is not easily shaken. Heroin is a high-priced private detective that follows you in cars that change color and model; a detective that taps your phone and photographs you from long distances with advanced camera equipment. Heroin interviews ex-girlfriends, old schoolmates, distant relatives, gathering information so that it always has something to hold against you. Heroin is extortion and blackmail and a litany of late seventies/early eighties gambits and scenarios.

It's a hard habit to shake.

But Bernie, being an unusual man, one day just stopped. It was just three months after they set a wedding date and two months before being terminated from his ambiguous position at the Art & Design Studio. Sophia just thought he'd gotten food poisoning, and he felt guilty when she took such good care of him when in fact he was going through withdrawal. It was one of the only instances in his life where he'd experienced a genuine emotion. Having gone over it numerous times, Bernie can't quite put his finger on what happened; all he's certain of is that he no longer uses heroin, and he doesn't miss it. But Bernie doesn't tell Sophia this. Because if Sophia and Bernie are both clean and sober, then the burden of equal effort will enter the relationship, which he's unprepared to shoulder.

Each day very early Sophia heads off to school to prepare class for who she affectionately calls her 'rental kids.' When she kisses Bernie's drowsy face goodbye and whispers loving reassurances in his ear, his face without permission from his mind forms an affectionate smile for his wife as she leaves to do her good work. Bernie then sleeps another hour before rising to face the day. His wife thinks this is when he is at work. He has the apartment to himself for hours, until exactly four-thirty when she comes home, happy but tired from her day, with cute tales of cute kids doing cute things.

Bernie eats a bowl of Raisin Bran, watches the news, shits, showers and settles into his time alone. His day looks like this, as it has since the very first day after he recovered from his heroin withdrawal.

He lays on the shag carpet floor of the living room. It was once a vibrant and sickening period-appropriate combination of

purple and orange swirls. It is now a far more optically forgiv-
ing matted grey and pink. Beside him lay a jug of water and a
glass, an ashtray, two packs of Marlboro Lights, a yellow lighter
(always yellow), a box of pills and a bottle of pills. There is a
stereo and television in the room, but they always remain off
when he's alone.

The first thing Bernie does after laying down and lighting a
cigarette is to take, propped up on one elbow, two one milligram
tabs of Clonazepam. Then he lays flat on his back and stares up
at the ceiling, smoking and ashing his cigarette with the familiar accuracy of repeated experience that only the blind tend to
know. Drowsiness sets in. Bernie fights it. After an hour or so, he
props himself up on his elbow again and reaches into the box for
a sleeping pill. An off-the-shelf sleeping pill called Nytol, which
contains the chemical Diphenhydramine Hydrochloride (rec-
ommended one pill an hour before sleep). He takes the glass of
water and swallows one down. He lights another cigarette since
he's already propped up, then lays back down on the floor. After
fifteen minutes, a crashing wave of sleep batters him around his
face and mind, but he keeps it at bay, something that years of
heroin use have given him a certain skill for. He repeats this each
hour, increasing the dose with each intake; two milligrams of
Clonazepam become four, one Nytol becomes two. He begins to
drink more water because of his intensely dry mouth. He always
prepares two packs of cigarettes, but he doesn't get around to
smoking many, because the drugs make smoking seem uninteresting. He's always slightly worried that one day he'll fall asleep
and light a fire. Bernie's greatest fear when it comes to death is
that of being burned alive.

In this way, he is a reasonable man.

Around one o'clock, death becomes the primary focus of
Bernie's mind. How much he'd like to die. (Not by burning
though). Much of his brain is unavailable to him, because it's

been called to duty elsewhere, keeping him awake. His entire focus is on not falling asleep and fantasizing about his own death.

A curious thing happens almost daily after the fourth cycle of pill consumption. Although Bernie and Sophia don't have a ceiling fan, a ceiling fan appears directly over Bernie's head. He can feel it cooling his face, which is a relief—the drugs make him warm and sweaty. After the fifth and penultimate cycle of Clonazepam and Nytol, Bernie watches as the ceiling fan disengages itself from the ceiling then, in slow-motion, descends towards his stupid and stupefied face. The ceiling fan oscillates six or so inches above him, so slowly that there isn't the typical blur we associate with ceiling fans. Bernie can make out all the mechanisms that have built the fan. He sees the blades and the rotor, as well as each individual screw.

Bernie's mind stays fixed on suicide, his eyes fixed on the fan. Then a very interesting thing begins to transpire. While Bernie smokes a Marlboro, the blade of the fan slices the ash of his cigarette off. Then it slices the cigarette in half. There is no sense of fear in Bernie, there is really no sense of anything in Bernie, because there is scarcely a trace of Bernie left. He watches as the tip of his nose is taken off and sent flying across the room, bouncing off the coffee table, rolling along the tile of the dining room floor until it comes to rest against the leg of the nearest dining table chair.

Then as Bernie abstractly fantasizes about various ways to kill himself—in a car, driving fast off a cliff or into a tree, with a gun at his temple or up inside of his mouth, leaping from a tall building or kicking away a chair on which he stands with a noose around his neck—the slowly moving fan begins to dissemble Bernie's very face and head, sending bloody chunks of himself all around the room.

This is when Bernie, each and every day, to his amazement, consumes the last of the pills he's set aside for himself. Amazed each time because as far he is aware in the moment, he has no face with which to consume the pills. Down go the Nytols, down the absurdly large large dose of Clonazepam. He's astonished to find a mouth in which to put a cigarette. Shocked to find himself drinking water with what he imagines to be a chasm of sinew and torn flesh, baffled by how the water does not fall out of his mouth and dampen the once gaudy, now faded shag carpet on which he's laying prostrate.

Bernie has not once looked in the mirror since he began this experiment.

He's understandably very sleepy in the period between the penultimate and last dose, or what Elvis called 'attacks.' It's during this period when it's hardest to stay awake. Yet Bernie's hallucination of the ceiling fan descending slowly to mutilate his visage is not a dream—he is not asleep. He knows so because he is smoking a cigarette. The blade of the fan moves so slowly that he's able to time the cigarette and get it into where he thinks his mouth is supposed to be. Bernie always wonders what kind of fan can be this sharp, that moving at what seems to be the pace of a cat sauntering down a hallway, it's still able to slice a cigarette in two. He begins to wonder about advancements in both fan technology and just how thinly metal can be sliced. Can it be sliced more thinly that the government is telling us? These are the things that jockey for space in Bernie's mind while the entire fiasco of facial disarticulation takes place.

After the lurid tango with the fan, Bernie will typically have what he believes to be a lucid dream. He knows he's not asleep during these dreams, as more than once the phone has rung or someone has knocked at the door during them. These dreams are Bernie's favorite part of the experience, because they pull him out of his fantasies of self-annihilation. He often finds himself in interesting or glamorous places, able to control how the narrative unfolds. Typically, the dreams involve things familiar to Bernie and his life: sometimes Sophia appears, or an ex-girlfriend, or a friend.

Today the dream is one he's had many times. A dream about driving. Obviously driving dreams, when it comes to dreams drawn from life, are much more exciting than ones of being at his aunt's house for Easter. Once he's in the car he can, to some extent, decide what type of trip he'll be taking. He hopes that over time his ability to control his lucid dreams will improve. Dreams of driving feel like some phantom has their hand on the steering wheel, and Bernie is doing his best to take control and make the turns and hit the gas. Sometimes the phantom is strong, sometimes weak. Today the dream is brief, and for the most part, Bernie is the one doing the driving. He never knows once it starts where he'll end up, and the dream always ends with no warning whatsoever.

In the dream, Bernie sees himself back in the bedroom, Sophia having just left for work. He thinks he has an appointment that he's late for. Out of the closet he chooses a casual brown corduroy sports coat and dark jeans. He brushes and washes that which needs brushing and washing, slips into a pair of loafers, splashes on some cologne and leaves the apartment to take the elevator down to the parking garage. It feels like a long time since he's left the apartment. The parking garage is half-full, and every single car there is a 1978 baby blue Volkswagen Golf, the car that he and Sophia had bought new four years ago. He walks to the nearest one and finds his key fits.

Now the illicit thrill of driving. A left turn out of the garage and he's assailed by the brutal sun. The universe is awake and alive. The car begins to move and he puts his hands on the wheel. He can't be certain if he's driving very fast or very slow. The world outside the car seems to speed up and slow down in a nauseating way. Children here, children there. A homeless person. Garbage swirling in the air caught in a spiral of wind under an overpass. A crosswalk. Smiling at the crossing guard. The turn signal, the turn. A woman's legs, distracting, facing forward; he's slightly out of his lane. Birds screaming and flying anarchically overhead. Imperceptibly small insects dying quickly and often as they collide with the windshield. Apartment buildings inside of which people are fucking and fighting, eating and weeping on the phone. A man is being stabbed somewhere he cannot see. A woman has been betrayed by another woman. Drugs and greasy money are exchanged with discreet hand movements in the doorways of bars. A man with a horribly sad life, who knows all his dreams are unattainable and prays each day he'll be one of those windshield bugs, smiles with difficulty wearing a used suit trying to sell used cars. The horrible reality of teenagers acting embarrassed by and smarter than their parents at shopping malls and doctor's offices. All the things Bernie associates with driving. The Kentucky Fried Chicken which signals the nearness of Dr. Morris. Bernie rolls his window down when he passes to take in the poultry breeze. One more turn, speed reduction, eyes scanning for empty spaces. A sequence of highly complex but now extraordinarily easy maneuvers and the car is parked. He lowers the car window, takes a cigarette out of the package in his left jacket pocket without taking the package itself out, lights the cigarette, turns off the ignition and leisurely smokes before flicking it out the window. Ignition back on, power windows up, ignition off, out of the car. The office becomes nearer and nearer to him as he moves forward.

'Mr. Phillips! It's been a while. I hope you're well, please take a seat Dr. Morris will see you shortly.'

This is the secretary, Pat. She smiles too often not realizing how frightening her false teeth look. Bernie wonders what her opinions of him and the other patients are. Surely, she hears the screams and weeping from the office while she does, what?

Crosswords? Each time he looks up from his magazine (Pen Collector) there's Pat, smiling back. It's possible that she never takes her eyes off Bernie, or she's developed an animal fast awareness of incoming eye contact and is always ready to meet it with a failing smile of comfort.

"Bernie, come in."

This is Dr. Morris himself now. Dr. Leslie Morris, as Bernie knows from the diplomas on the wall. Dr. Morris is bald. This comforts Bernie because it means his doctor is familiar with real and profound suffering. He wears stylishly crumpled linen suits and smokes languidly with his head slightly tilted in a way they surely must teach you when studying psychiatry. He's a good enough psychiatrist. Bernie can attest to this based solely on his large amounts of prescribed Clonazepam.

"I was happy to hear you'd—please sit down Bernie. Why would you smell a plant? I was happy to hear you'd made an appointment Bernie. I was worried you were giving up on therapy. And as your doctor I can assure you, you are not one who can give up on therapy. You're a deeply ill man Bernie, and the problems you contend with are not going to resolve themselves without the help of someone with training such as I've received."

"For fuck sake Doc you've never said I was 'deeply ill' before. Jesus, did they teach you bedside manners?"

"This isn't palliative care Bernie."

"Fine. I think I do okay for the most part."

"You don't do okay for the most part Bernie, not at all. The fact that you think you're doing okay for the most part is proof of how delusional and unhealthy your mind is. "

"I don't think I like—"

"So, what prompted you to come back and see me Bernie. Tell me what's on your mind."

Bernie feels compelled to smash Doctor Morris' phone over his head and walk out, but he realizes he'll be bored for the rest of the day, plus probably no more Clonazepam. He watches the thought leave his mind.

"Listen Doctor. Do people ever say that, Listen Doctor? Like that? It sounds wrong. Listen Doc. Doc?"

Then Bernie, whose eyes were never closed, feels the back of his head on the rug and realizes the dream is over.

Once the final pills are consumed Sophia will be home in exactly one hour. Anyone who might happen to come into the room would see the following: a man of average height and weight, middle aged, not particularly striking but not unattractive, lay-ing on his back in the centre of his living room on a shag rug. A man wearing charcoal grey flannel slacks and a white dress shirt with the first three buttons undone. Wearing socks but shoe-less. Sweat-drenched. No pillow under his head, no blanket over his body. Two packages of Marlboro Lights, a jug of water and a glass, a chunky crystal ashtray containing many half-smoked cigarettes, a pill bottle and a small colorful box. That is all they'd see. If they were to come into the room and stand over Bernie, they would see his grey eyes fixed with almost religious tran-quility directly at the ceiling above him, eyes full of both sweat and tears. They would see him occasionally smile, the way one smiles when watching children play in a pile of raked leaves mid-autumn. A smile of beatific innocence that conveys a sense of peace, the smile of a man who is made happy seeing the late afternoon light flickering off a flattened lake.

Slowly, the ceiling fan begins to ascend from where Bernie feels it to be—lodged directly inside his skull—up to where it belongs. Bernie watches as his nose rises slowly from the floor adjacent to where he's lying and comes as if invited by his head to reposition itself where it belongs. Small pieces of flesh do similar things. Bernie is often reminded of a sort of snowy chum in reverse, red flakes of tissue settling upon his face and creating a pile, a pile called Bernie. Within thirty minutes Bernie is returned to the man he was when he sat and ate cereal and watched the news. He gets up, very sleepy still, and gathers what's left on the floor. He puts the pills back in the cabinet. He drinks all the water left in the jug directly from it, then puts the jug and the glass in the sink to be cleaned later. In the bathroom, without looking in the mirror, he washes his face vigorously, still stunned to feel his nose. He combs his hair and puts on a new dress shirt. There is a briefcase he keeps by the door. He opens it and rearranges the various papers and files as he does every day, just so that were Sophia to look into it (she never would) she'd see there'd been changes, work had been done, files attended to.

Sophia will be home within five minutes now. Bernie pours himself a gin and tonic, sits on the couch and turns on the television to watch the early news. As precise as ever, he hears Sophia turn the key in the lock and come in.

"Bernie, darling are you home?"

"Yes sweetheart. I just got in myself, just fixed a drink."

Sophia comes into the living room after taking off her shoes. Bernie inclines his head to look back at her and smiles. She holds it in her two hands and kisses him on his forehead.

"You okay baby? You look tired. Is it work or are you trying to taper again?"

"No darling I'm not trying to taper, not now. Things are too hectic at work. I can't deal with feeling sick while I have this much work on my plate."

"That's okay baby" Sophia says "Remember there's no rush. You can do it when you're ready and I'll be here to support you. I love you. What you want to do isn't easy, but hey, at least you're willing to admit it's something that needs to change right?"

Bernie pulls her around to his side of the couch with his hand and she sits beside him. He maneuvers her legs onto his lap and rubs her feet. She smiles at him and he smiles back. He hands her his gin and tonic and watches her take a sip. He feels a rush of love for his wife.

"Let's see what the fuck is going on in the news Bernie, the world is so up its own ass right now."

While Bernie and Sophia watch the news, Bernie looks up at where the ceiling fan had been not an hour ago, and suppresses a slight smile.

LETTERS FROM THE BATTLEFIELD

Richard Masterson, July 2, 2016—Sending me to a better place. I am alright with this. We have to live and die by the choices that we make. I have made mine. I love you Renee. I am gonna carry your heart. Always carry my heart in your heart...

Michael Yowell, January 3,, 2016—I love you. To Gerald: you're a zero. I love you Mandy, Tiffany. I love you, too.

1.

Dear Lazara,

2073 is not the finest year. You look lovely as always, eighty-seven years old today. I started this project at forty-four. I wrote the first of the following letters that year, in 2017, when this idea came to me, then I wrote you another when I got sick the second time; when death felt near, in other words, last week. I'm sick, but I'm smarter, and I know better what I'd intended this to be. I'm tapping this out with the single finger my last stroke didn't render useless. I'll be ninety-nine in six weeks, as I promised you I would be a long time ago. "I'll do ninety-nine for you," I'd say. You've always been so terrified that I might die before you. I've tried to be strong. I can see you from my rocking chair now, whispering to tired succulents, spraying our hyacinths with that bottle whose nozzle we once joked resembled a duck.

I love you.

October 14, 2017

Dear Audrey,

Do you remember when we finally met in real life? We'd been talking obsessively online, then I came to Manhattan to meet and abduct you. We kissed for the first time in a strange Airbnb-ers apartment while she noisily taught herself guitar via YouTube. The next morning, we disappeared into that cottage upstate.

You do remember. Over the next twelve days we fucked ourselves into a mess of painful, damaged organs. In such short time we covered a urinary tract infection, a trip to a jenky hospital and a prescription for unguents. A nurse with neck and hand tattoos asked you where you'd been spending your time. From the bathroom, you sent me a DM on Instagram of yourself smiling, holding your urine sample. The sacred DM. A technological envelope that changed our lives.

After two days of antibiotics you had a yeast infection I insisted you pass onto me in lieu of a condom. I couldn't bear a layer of latex coming between us with so little time left. I can still see the September light through the blinds, slicing up your naked body while you lay on your back. Your body, so many lines; your stomach falling into a shallow made by your ribs, pelvis and hips. I applied the ointment to your vagina. I think you photographed it. Then you put the ointment on me; you so tender with my foreskin. We traversed so many levels of intimacy in not even two weeks.

The final day of our being together, we got to Port Authority forty-five minutes before the bus left for Newark Airport. Carrying our heavy bags, we managed to find two grimy sex shops. We wanted to fuck one last time so badly. I remember being in awe of you, how fearless you were, walking into those places asking if they had "buddy rooms"—a term I'd never heard before. You wanted to squeeze into a cubicle with a peep show or coin-powered porn clips so we could fuck in a filthy cum-splattered box. I fell doubly in love with you then. They wouldn't let us go into a room together and I remember how your face fell. On the bus to Newark you gently held my sore cock in your mouth, pretending to sleep on my lap, then we scoured the airport for a bathroom we could use. We tried a handicapped one, but the floor was covered in shit. We found a family bathroom with a diaper changing table, but the door wouldn't lock. We must have looked like we were late for our flight the way we were scrambling around.

Eventually, we went back outside. It was so hot that day. We walked past the taxi and limo stands and found a scorching hot silver electrical box next to the exit road. I thought for sure security would see us. I was looking for them everywhere. You squatted on the ground, rubbing my cock through my pants with one hand, slathering coconut oil between your legs with the other. I think we laughed when you took my cock out. We were both so sore, so destroyed. Then you stood up, lifting your dress so anyone watching could see your perfect ass, and you leaned over yourself, grabbing your ankles with your hands. You looked like a lurid, shaking triangle. We fucked there, your head down, looking up at me between your legs. You moved for the both of us. I held your breast with one hand and steadied myself against the burning box with the other. I scanned for cops. Neither of us came, but neither did security. We weren't aiming for orgasms, we just didn't want to be separated. I wouldn't see you again until I had money to get to London, where you were starting your masters. You took off the panties you'd been wearing, balled them up, and pressed them into my hand. "Don't forget me" you said. But I couldn't.

We limped back to the departure gate and I waved you goodbye. Your eyes were wet but you did not cry. I was scared to see you go. You were too real. Surely, you would die in a crash or forget me. I allowed one tear to to exit my left eye then took the bus back to the city.

You know that I've always been interested in the experiences of people who know the exact moment they'll die. Outside of horrific beheadings, choreographed murders, and holocaustic lineups in front of pre-dug holes, it tends only to be people exe-cuted by the state, those freed from their suffering by euthanasia, or the suicidal who are privy to this information.

When I took my first vacation after rehab, I went back to Vancouver to see Aaron. We had plans for revenge and nostalgia in the city, but we wanted to go camping first. The mushrooms we ate that night were from God, and in the mountains we lost language. Staring up from an earth bed we'd made, this strangely relaxed squirrel whose tail went back and forth like a metro-nome, beeping with each movement, had us convinced he was providing our Wi-Fi.

Back in the city, we spent the night at the Patricia Hotel. We talked about a lot of things, so we talked about suicide. Unlike the Aaron I'd always known, he now said that suicide was selfish. His brother had died suddenly eight months prior, so I under-stood his change of heart. But my heart remained unchanged.

We lay beside each other in one of two twin beds, nibbling on hallucinogens and painfully sunburnt, our clammy bodies pressed together, discussing how it's only suicidal people who leave notes for their loved ones. We said that we—that everyone, really—should write letters to family and friends in advance, knowing that one day we will die. We'd both been profoundly wounded by losing someone close to us, and we agreed that we would have felt comforted if that person had at least left us something to read.

The next morning Aaron went home to his new wife. Staring at the junkies from my hotel room window, some of whom I rec-ognized, I remembered something beautiful and sad. I remem-bered that before I left, you and I watched *Saving Private Ryan*, and Matt Damon did something I stupidly thought Aaron and I had invented—he'd pulled a letter from the corpse of a dead soldier before running back into battle. A letter intended for the dead soldier's family. My grandfather had probably carried such a letter at Dunkirk. I had always known this—soldiers in war carry letters with their gear, letters for those who pray each night that they'll never receive such a letter.

Life hasn't been easy for you. I've never known anyone who found it easy. Others have had it far worse than we did. But the pain we knew was real. It was ours, and it was precious to us. Those gems made of trauma in some ways stood in for the children we knew we didn't want. At times, we let the pain become monstrous and burrow inside us, creating more wounds, and at others, we let it become something beautiful that taught us, vanishing like steam on a bathroom mirror, leaving a trace to remind you it was there.

When people say "Life is war" I think they're exaggerating. It's difficult, sure, but I've never heard of battlefields awash with the beauty I've seen and experienced. The sense of life as burden is the whiny privilege of youth, and as I've aged, my gratitude has eclipsed my resentment.

So, I think it's soldiers who've been doing what I want to do now. More than executed prisoners, more than self-annihilators, each of whose last words are infected by agendas. What makes us lucky is that—to hijack a metaphor that doesn't exactly fit—we've been diving into foxholes, dodging sniper fire, and running for our lives *together*.

So, I wrote a letter from the battlefield for you. I'm sorry I can't change the reason it's in your hands. It's in your hands because I've passed away before you, and you found this envelope when the bank let you open my safety deposit box.

I'm sorry that I'm gone. Chances are the chemotherapy didn't work, or I got ran over while I crossed the street eating yogurt and daydreaming, or an air-conditioner fell on my head, or I opened my big mouth in the wrong place. Or, since we've been watching spy movies lately, I was walking home late—it must've been fall—hands pushed deep into the pockets of my overcoat, when I was taken out by a sniper, mistaken for a Russian spy who had too many secrets to live. It's hard to say. I'm only forty-four. I guess how doesn't matter. You'll be painfully familiar with that part. I want to console you, but I am not sure of the right thing to say. I'm not sure if there is a right thing to say.

Probably you're feeling like you can't go on.

You can.

Remember you were happy. I've seen the photos. You were laughing and alive, enjoying your life long before you met me. You can enjoy it now that I'm gone. I know that's not much comfort right now. That right now you feel alone. You're not.

The dead are always available to us, just not how we'd prefer. I'm not with you the way you want, but I am with you. If you look for me, you'll find me. You can find me in everything that was important to me. You can find me if you push your hair behind your ear with one finger, gently, the way I used to. You can find me in that tree on Palmerston we loved, in the succulents at Allan Gardens.

After my first overdose, I stopped fearing death. That lack of fear caused a lot of problems for a while. I never understood why I had survived when so many other people hadn't. I know I'm not special. But when I met you, I thought it was possible I survived just to find you. I know we were together in another life. I know I searched for you all throughout this one. I searched for you in every woman. In every city, every drink, every drug, every long exhale.

I searched for you in clichés.

Imagine how open your pores become after a hot shower. Now imagine your mind and your heart as those pores. You can absorb me. You can touch me. I am the vapor that follows you everywhere like a shadow. I can fill you up if you become a vessel. I've never met a woman as strong as you. Be that strong now. I've simply left one waiting room for another. And when you die, I'll be there, leafing through a copy of *Pen Collector*. I can't explain how I know this. You need to trust me now more than ever before. Be fresh out of the shower, all the time.

Don't let them bury me in anything but a pair of Adidas sweatpants and a white t-shirt.

Don't let them bury me in anything but a pair of Adidas sweatpants and a white t-shirt, turned into a pocketful of ash.

If I'm still a working artist, and someone wants to print a statement about my death, give them this: "His missing son, his bedroom untouched, a museum of grief, his art career."

I didn't believe in the possibility of an honest relationship until I met you. Women had told me before that they didn't believe in monogamy, but I always suspected they were saying it for my sake. And inevitably the first time I'd fuck someone else, they weren't as okay with it as they'd said or thought they would be. I was relieved the first time I fucked someone else and it wasn't a problem. I was even more relieved the first time you fucked someone else in Munich. I always loved when you described to me what it had been like fucking this man or that woman. Your opposition to monogamy and your interests in _____, _____ sex—all of it felt like I should pinch myself. I had trouble believing you were real.

I could tell you anything and you never judged me. I could tell you I had unappealing instincts. You helped me fulfill many longstanding desires, one of which was when you had sex with me on top of my father's grave in the middle of the afternoon. I wanted to avenge my inappropriate exposure to sex at a too-young age, something that fucked my brain up. I longed to punish him, while he lay in a mouldering heap of teeth and hair and his own black karma six feet beneath us, having sex with someone who he would have wanted.

All my desires were arousing to you, as yours were to me.

It's not only what you did for me, or were for me. It was the way you moved through life slowly but confidently, mindful of your footprints but still intent on leaving a mark. You had an aloof detachment from your career, something that took me years to learn. You were quietly ambitious, wanting only to be more than comfortable. You didn't want your face on the cover of a magazine.

Before we met, when you were living in China, you showed me an early video you'd made where you punished a banana in high heels and an ill-fitting wig. Somehow it spoke to my mind's native language. Everything you created worked on me like neurosurgery, either recalibrating or validating my brain. The way I wanted my work to affect others was how your work affected me. You wrote and made things I wished I'd written and made. I'd only ever felt this before with dead people. I'd always held my nose up at poetry. I thought nothing good came after Anne Sexton and Philip Larkin. I was wrong. You wrote poems as short or shorter than Issa's and Basho's, but they were about more than mosquitos, reeds and the wind. Later, in person, you told me you sometimes felt like a baby bird, stunned flying into the glass of each new day, who I'd warm back to life, cradled in my large hands.

Beyond all of these nameable realms lies the inarticulable bulk of life. As a woman, your hand matched the hand I'd held flat against the window of the world all my life. At first, we could only trace words and shapes together in technological unison, across a vast tract of the world I was growing to resent. But once we were behind the same window, we linked our hands and drew on the glass when we felt like it, leaving our obscure signature. Often we spurned the window for a tent, creating our own cornily romantic world under one duvet, one umbrella, one small patch of sky we claimed as our front yard.

Up to this day, I've never been happier to watch a human being breathe. Everything I once scorned as saccharine I now savor because it is so. Everything I once felt bothered by, I now have difficulty bringing into focus.

I love you.

January 3, 2073

Dear Lazara,

I'll be ninety-nine in less than two months. I've been sick again, for just over a year now, and you've been like Katniss Everdeen. I never thought anyone could have such fortitude. It doesn't take much to slip slowly into a grave, but it takes everything to hold the slipping hand. I don't know what to say that I haven't by now, except that I'm sorry it took so long to write you another letter. One beautiful thing about terminal illness is that you're given time to talk to the people you love before you go. And you are the only person I love still alive. We've spent each night beside each other in bed, talking until we fell asleep. I can't imagine what it was like the morning I didn't wake up. Before I came back to this project, I looked at what I wrote you in my forties. I said a lot of what I've been saying to you recently. Look at all of it when you're ready, it explains what you're reading.

In the fifty-nine years I've known you, you've been so incredibly strong. Strong without losing your softness. I cherish the paradox of you. This time I got sick it was obvious I wouldn't recover. Nobody is meant to be this old. The doctors could only make me more comfortable. Morphine's been one way. You've been far more effective.

Thank you for taking me out of the hospital. I wanted this to happen in our home. The fact that we have a home is amazing; in fact, we have two. It seemed impossible fifty years ago. Now we have this house on a street canopied by trees, and the place in New Jersey. Everything we've ever wanted or needed the universe has provided, right from the beginning. Starting with those twelve days in the cottage. I sort of wish this could end back there, in Rosendale. The sky was so much bigger there. I want to hear bird songs that harmonize with my tinnitus, not streetcars and sirens.

I pull this laptop out each afternoon when you fall asleep in the chair beside me. I want to get as much down as I can, but it's slow work with my single finger. Soon Vera will come to change me, and you'll zombie-walk from the chair to bed. You'll either wake up and we'll talk, or you'll just mumble "I love you." Then I'll turn on my right side, put my left hand under your right breast, and we'll sleep, just the way we've slept every night for almost six decades. You used to say, "I look forward to sleeping with you." I loved it too, the way we fit. Every place I'm hollow you protrude; where you protrude I'm hollow. Every angle of your body matches mine like we came in parts to be assembled as one. That made it easy for us to pretend we were siblings, back when we used to do that. We've never had to readjust in bed, we've never slept on our backs or done that television thing of saying goodnight then turning away from each other. I imagine some marriages are like that. I never forget how rare our marriage is. How lucky we have been and are.

Thinking of what I could write to you, I realized I'd forgotten something entirely. I always feared that some obscure, private experience of mine would repulse you. But were our roles reversed, I'd be thrilled to learn anything new about you.

I'll start with something innocent. As a child, when my parents were still married (I must have been eight or nine), I saw what I think was a movie on television late one night. I had a TV in my bed. Television was my most reliable parent. Over time I came to wonder if I actually did see this on TV or not, because throughout my twenties I scoured the internet to find anything about it and had no luck.

From what I recall, the movie was a single scene that repeated with minor variations. Two men would take an enormous mirror, twenty by twenty feet, to the end of a highway that was under construction. The highway dropped off into an endless gorge. Each man would hold one end of the mirror, then slowly they'd slide it onto the highway and stand there holding it in place. A car would then appear. Sometimes I remember the view being from within the car, other times I remember it differently. There would be a happy couple in the car, a man driving while his girlfriend lay her head on his shoulder. As they drove, a pair of headlights would appear in the far distance ahead of them. At first it wasn't a big deal. But then as the headlights got closer, the driver would swerve, only to have the approaching headlights swerve in the same direction. The driver would get more and more frantic. The girlfriend would scream. Then when the opposing headlights couldn't be any closer, the car would crash through the mirror, off the cliff, then explode in the distance. They'd been manipulated into playing a game of chicken with their own reflection.

The men would disappear off screen, then return with another twenty-by-twenty foot mirror. They'd put it in place again and wait until another car came. One always did. The action would repeat, the mirror would shatter, the car would explode, the men would bring out a new mirror. I remember thinking that I'd never seen a movie so simple, so much like early video games I was playing at the time.

I've wondered if my mind was trying to warn me of the mental illness I'd soon become acquainted with. I came close to death playing chicken with myself more than once.

*

I don't like the other thing I've never told you.

I've had insomnia all my life. When we met I was taking 200 milligrams of Trazodone, a heavy dosage. But the truth is, when my doctor got me up to 50 milligrams in 2006, it worked like a charm, and I never had trouble sleeping again. I noticed that I dreamt less, and what dreams I did have were hard to remember. I liked this. I met someone on Facebook in 2008 who was also taking it, and I asked them about their dreams. They told me that they'd had the same experience at 50 milligrams, but it wasn't a high enough dosage to put them to sleep. When they found the dose that worked, 200 milligrams, one side effect was that they never dreamt again. I've told you that I never dream and it's true. What's not true is that I've never dreamt, which is something I think I led you to believe. The dream I'm going to describe was one I'd had since I was a small child. By 2008, when I was seeking ways to stop dreaming, it had become my single dream, and it recurred often.

Why would someone be given a single dream, after experiencing the typical myriad nonsense narratives while asleep for most of their lives?

I did not like the dream God gave me.

I had always been an expert at manipulating doctors, and when this guy on Facebook told me about the dreamless coma of 200 milligrams of Trazodone, I informed my doctor that my current dosage wasn't working. Eventually I got up to 200, and it worked like a charm. By the time we met in 2014, I hadn't had a single dream in six years.

I'd been having this dream my entire life until then. It traumatized me in different ways depending on my age.

I was sitting at a big mahogany desk on the top floor of a stark concrete high-rise. The building was long and narrow. Maybe fifteen feet across but hundreds of feet ahead of me. This was my office. There were cracks in the wall, through which slanted light Catholicized dead skin, dust and smoke. A shitty desk lamp provided the only other light. I was mostly alone and never spoke. Pigeons murmured, their tattered wings occasionally morphing into quick bright triangles. I was unable to see the opposite end of my floor, it narrowed to infinity. I felt scared of whatever was ahead of me. I smoked cigarettes and rearranged blank papers at my desk. Faceless people brought me things silently and deferentially, backing out with bowed heads. I counted at least fifteen floors in this building, most of which I knew nothing about.

The floor beneath my office was occupied, standing room only, with what appeared to be high-level athletes of every sport I was once good at. The athletes would jog and stretch, practice their swings and shots. I would often see myself among them, at whatever age I was best at each sport. A seventeen-year-old me, gangly and pale, practicing three-pointers. Me at fifteen, stretching my hamstrings with a pocket full of tennis balls; at twelve, fiddling with a squash racket. I didn't need to analyze this floor. These were obviously my alternate destinies had I not let my desire to modify my perception overpower my desire to turn my body into a machine.

The floor beneath the sports floor was full of flowers, floor to ceiling. Dozens of men and women in hazmat suits extracted fluid from these flowers with long syringes. There were numerous species, none of which I recognized. All of them looked menacing and overripe, pulsating and fleshy. They resembled flowers as meat, painted by Soutine. The fluid they produced was to be used either medicinally, or narcotically. That it lay directly beneath the sports floor was not lost on me.

The floor beneath the sketchy greenhouse I never saw.

The floor beneath the floor I never saw made no sense logically, and was occupied solely by cars crashing into each other at high speed, head on. They never stopped crashing and they never stopped driving. They neither broke down nor reassembled.

Somehow they remained in a state of constant pre- and post-collision. The noise was deafening and the room stunk of grease and scorched rubber. I'd spend time standing at the doorway while vehicles pulverized each other inches from my face. I never saw any drivers. I never saw the pink clouds of tissue, or the sprayed blood and splintered bone.

There were four floors I never saw, but sensed were occupied by dim sum restaurants of world-class quality.

The next floor was populated by one mid-to-late adolescent girl. The girl always changed and I never saw the same girl twice. Even now I feel the need to remind you that the dream was beyond my control, so deep is the shame this floor instilled in me. The girl stood alone under a spotlight, shifting her weight from foot to foot and looking around idly. Each girl was thin and gangly. Their skin was shiny and tight, as if the velocity of their pubescence was urgently altering the shape of their bodies; widening their hips, imposing their volume on other body parts. That they never sought me out with their eyes was a relief. I recognized this floor. I was raised to believe dreams are meaningless, and that meaninglessness is immune to morality, but while I never interacted with any of these shiny girls—and I tried to suppress my arousal at the sight of them; never masturbated to the memory of the dream but instead woke up nauseous, shuddering with self-loathing—I still found it difficult not to feel disgusting, as if I'd done something terribly wrong.

The floor beneath the nubile girl was littered with hideously old and decrepit elderly couples. Older than old, they looked to be one-hundred-and-thirty at least, resembling undulating piles of Chinatown garbage. They'd slowly crawl after each other on scabrous hands and knees across a concrete floor, fruitlessly attempting to grasp at body parts just out of reach. Grotesque genitals, scrotums like roadkill, breasts like deflated balloons, varicostic limbs—anything distended they might grab onto. It was a futile, disgusting display. Spiting nature by living, they'd moan and grunt as they scrambled along the floor, their baroque, rheumatic hands never able to reach one another.

Beneath that floor was one I never saw but often heard. Although I had no knowledge of classical music whatsoever, I was aware that this floor contained every single instrument from a standard symphony, each playing the same expertly-sustained mezzo piano D-flat without pause. At other times the floor was silent.

Underneath the harmonic floor was a floor that contained the world's largest crib. Sitting in the middle was a man who looked like my father, naked except for a diaper, a mustache, and a gold chain adorned with both a crucifix and the Star of David. He would scream unrelentingly like a colicky infant. Whenever I was with this baby-man I'd have a soother in my hand. The sound of his voice was horrible, and I'd try to toss the soother at him to silence the room, but I couldn't move my arm. I tried to spend as little time as possible on this floor.

The lowest floor I assumed to be at ground level. Although I never saw who was on it, I knew it to be one long lineup of people I'd wronged throughout my life. As a child this confused me, but I'm certain that back then it was a line of angry women, bitter strangers and estranged friends from my future. In my thirties, it hadn't grown any longer than it was when I was nine. During my time on the West Coast I came to understand this floor as an example of pratityasamutpada, dependent origination, and felt I'd have to meditate for countless lifetimes to shorten the line of those who had grievances with me. That, or find a way to put an end to dreaming altogether.

Sometimes I wonder if this is the building I was born in, or if I built this structure in my mind for reasons that, as a ninety-eight-year-old man, I still don't understand. It's a dream that's taught me nothing other than what I've always known.

*

The rest of Brad Phillips you are intimately familiar with. You were the most important part of my life, and often the only thing that kept me interested in continuing the cycle of sleep and reanimation.

Again, I'm so sorry you're reading this. We often spoke when we were young of dying at the exact same moment. Of course we knew this couldn't happen. Last night, I thought, the expression that we're all living on borrowed time, well really, it's all borrowed time from the minute we escape from our mother's bodies. Even if we never asked to borrow it, to be in such a heavy debt. In that way, it's a miracle we're still together at this age, neither of us having been clipped by a bus, infantilized by dementia or dropped by the bolt of an aneurysm.

You cured me. You didn't see me as a project that needed fixing, or a malady that required a remedy. You saw me, you touched me, you didn't back away from the parts of me that weren't soft or smooth, but rubbed your hand against them and told me you loved them.

I've put myself in your position, and probably you're feeling like you can't go on. Probably I've said this already. You can go on. Remember that you were happy. I've seen the photos. You were enjoying your life long before you met me. You can do that still. You're not alone.

I can't tell if I fell asleep or if a week's passed. Time is a kind of magic trick. I learned that the first time I got sick. Soon, time will stop for me. An hour ago you came in from the garden to wash the pollen stains from your fingers. Vera was rubbing my legs and my eyes were half closed. You leaned into me and whispered "dog style" in my ear. You watched my eyes open and smile, then went on your way. I don't know how long ago it was that you said "dog style" was way dirtier than "doggy style," but I've always thought it was hilarious. It'd make me laugh during sex when you said you wanted it dog style, and then you'd laugh too, and we'd end up in a naked fit of laughter. You'd also ask me if I wanted to "do the numbers" because we both thought the term "sixty-nine" was so stupid. Even though I can't be anything close to sexual at this point, those memories feel like sex and they're precious. They remind me of all the fun we had in beds and parks and hotels throughout the world.

I'm running out of things to say Lazara, as well as the energy to get them down. My own experience with death is that it takes time for the absence to really hit you, to establish its unprecedented hunger. There is the primordial scream once it registers, where you don't recognize the animal sounds issuing from your mouth. Then that absence strangely becomes a presence. A volume of grief that establishes a heavy space inside the body.

Stay alert. Don't let grief steal your days. Look for me in the remainder of your time here, and in whatever comes next. I will be searching for you in every pocket of space, every envelope of time. I will hunt you down like a leopard hunts a gazelle. Roll gently onto your back for me, and know my teeth are made of feathers.

I love you Lazara.

2.

I finished the letter and gave it to my lawyer one week before my ninety-ninth birthday. I knew I had very little time left. I could smell it. I could smell *me*. Lazara had been assisting Vera in caring for me, working in our garden, and managing to both write poems and make paintings. She seemed as if she'd never die.

Three days later, the day before my birthday, I watched from my bed as she worked in the garden, cutting back dead leaves to expose healthy nodes the sun could infiltrate. I thought she was taking a break when I saw her slump into the grass. She was not talking a break. She was eighty-eight that afternoon, much older than she'd ever expected to be.

Brains give up, refuse to continue, go on strike. I learned that when the doctor came. She'd suffered a stroke so vicious it had put her in a coma instantly. I felt crushed, but also relieved that she wouldn't have to continue watching me suffer.

We had the same lawyer, and knowing how sick I was, how sick Lazara was at this point, he brought the contents of both our safety deposit boxes to my bed the next day. I put my finished letter in an envelope, managed to write the letter 'A' on it by holding a pen in my mouth, and placed it amongst my belongings. In case she miraculously came out of her coma. In case that happened after I died.

I wept looking through what she'd felt was worth keeping. Amongst jewelry I'd given her, bits of dried flowers, and letters I sent her when she was a grad student, I found a yellowed envelope. It said, "Dear Brad" in the steady handwriting that had long since abandoned her.

I opened it immediately and began to read with the help of a magnifying glass:

October 14, 2017

Dear Brad,

You left four nights ago for Vancouver to see Aaron. For some reason, today I had an idea. I was thinking about a war movie we watched last week. Saving Private Ryan. *I thought it was beautiful (not the film so much, which was standard Spielberg shlock), if sad, the way soldiers carry around letters to their loved ones in case they're killed in battle, and I realized that really, nobody does this. It dawned on me on that maybe everyone should. Because I know that if you died, I'd want to hear from you. I'd be starved for anything you left behind. So, I'm writing this now, to tell you what you mean to me, so that if I die before you, you'll have something to be comforted by...*

I managed a few visits to the hospital with the help of the nurses after Lazara's stroke. The doctors told me that comas like these, especially at her age, were akin to death. All that remained were sparks of electricity that would travel throughout her body seeking a non-existent exit. She couldn't breathe or eat without tubes and machines. She was living what both of us feared most, and I knew that she was in there, listening, scared and pissed off. The doctors and paperwork and legalities of "end of life protocols" through the hospital would be tedious and clinical. Lazara and I had no living wills, but we'd discussed our shared desires about situations such as these, hoping that they would never occur. On my third visit, I called my lawyer, and within two days Lazara was at home with me, her garden already doing things I knew she'd prefer it not do. Vera helped greatly then, and a hospital bed was brought into our home and placed next to the double bed I'd been dying in for what felt like years. While I was hooked up solely to a morphine drip I could remove and reinsert at will, Lazara required arachnoid tubes and IV's to keep her alive, if alive is what she was. Her doctor called daily to tell me she required hospitalization, and each time I would hand the phone to Vera to hang up, not having said a word.

I hired a private nurse, as Vera herself was not young and had enough trouble changing and bathing me. This nurse came three times a day, and did for Lazara what Vera did for me and more: rolling her to avoid bedsores, changing her IV, re-intubating her with fresh tubes pulled from ultra-modern packages. I tried the things one tries. I sung to Lazara, squeezed her hand, whispered memories into her ears. Nothing worked. It was clear to me she wasn't going to pull a DeNiro from *Awakenings* and sit up in bed, asking for a toothbrush.

Gradually, I became aware of a much gentler way I could honor our youthful dream of dying simultaneously. At this point I was already ninety-nine, and had fulfilled one promise I'd never fathomed would come true.

So one Friday I told Vera she could leave early, which I'd never done before. I saw a tear stream down her face when she kissed my forehead goodbye. It was the first time Lazara and I had been alone in our home in over a year.

It wasn't as hard as I'd thought it would be, although I admit I had very little physical strength. I managed to swing my feet over the side of my bed, and then, grasping the bar of hers, I pulled myself up, crawling into bed with Lazara one last time. Although I only had a single finger dextrous enough to type with, the rest of my hands could form rudimentary shapes. Of course, it would have been impossible if her face displayed any of the emotion that mine was still capable of, but hers was frozen, staring at me and right through me at once. I lay curled beside her for quite a while, holding her the way I did each night for over half a century. I kissed her forehead, her eyes, her mouth. I wept unrestrainedly for a good two minutes. Then I reached across to my bed and grabbed my pillow. I took the breathing tube from her nose, which set off a high-pitched beep that somehow matched the tone of my tinnitus. I found that soothing. I managed to lay on my back without pushing her off the bed. After one more kiss, I put my pillow over my face. Then I managed to pull her body so that she was laying on top of me, and I put her face directly on the pillow I'd used to cover mine. I wrapped my arms around the pillow so that I was holding the back of Lazara's head. Then I hugged my wife with all the strength I had left in my body.

I felt myself gasping for air. I felt my legs twitch, but I held on tight. I hugged her head and forced my face into the pillow. I could feel the outline of her jaw, the protrusion of her nose pressing against mine. My body fought because my body always has, but I was determined to honor my wife's longstanding wish. I was determined that we leave together; I thought it would make it easier for us to find each other afterward. My body submitted to my will and I stopped twitching. I felt my hands release their grip on the back of her head. I heard the beep of the machine, I heard my tinnitus, and then I heard Lazaras's voice, as clear and strong as it had ever been.

"How long have you been waiting?" she said. "I'm so happy to see you. I wrote you a letter you know."

I did hear that, her soft voice, telling me how happy she was to see me. Telling me about the letter. Then I heard myself sputter and cough. My body jerked a bit, and I pulled the pillow away from my face.

Lazara was there, underneath me. She looked the same as she had ten minutes ago, but this time she was dead. It had worked, but not how I meant it to. It hadn't worked at all.

I gave Vera the rest of the week off. I'd have time to catch up to Lazara. I just needed a little ingenuity and the right combination of medications, of which there were dozens to choose from.

DEEP WATER

N THE FALL OF 1996 I WAS AS BUSY AS I'D EVER BEEN before in my young life. I was into the second week of my longest period of abstention from opiates when my father committed suicide by overdosing on heroin, thereby confirming the genetic legacy I had been attempting to refute in my period of sobriety. I began to display the symptoms of two extremely painful and awfully hard to diagnose diseases at the same time. I had been kicked out of art school and was attempting to give it another shot at a more relaxed, tuition-negotiable, semi-private art institution. I was treated as a minor prodigy there, which at twenty-two led to the inflation of my ego, causing me to attend irregularly and smoke openly in figure drawing class. I had discovered that a great deal of change can occur in both mind and body when one deprives oneself of sleep, and was taking these experiments quite far. My small group of friends were all similarly anti-social, autodidactic, talented, and at war with the permanence of their bodies. It was a good time.

What happened though is that, in fact, it wasn't a good time. Truthfully, it was a very bad time. My father, who I loved, had taken his own life. I'd said horrible things to him the last time we spoke. I was in shocking pain that would come from nowhere throughout the day and disappear just as mysteriously. Stunning pain that led me to believe I was suffering heart attacks, strokes, spontaneously breaking bones. Although this sounds like I was suffering from anxiety, I was not. This doesn't mean that I didn't also suffer from anxiety. I later learned out what I *was* suffering from, and then suffered further from the knowledge and practical reality of those illnesses.

So, I disappeared. What makes my case different from most cases, is that I was unaware I'd disappeared, and had never intended to. Oh, you might think that I'd say 'Hey, it was easy for me disappear, because nobody cared about me enough to look for me.' But I won't. What happened is that I'd done such a stellar job of pushing people away and making it clear I didn't want them to care about me, that they took me seriously and continued to enjoy their youth.

I was gone for two months. I know now that my mother *did* worry, and would call the woman I was dating at the time, Yasmin, who could only reassure her by saying that, "Well, sometimes Brad *does* disappear. But he always comes home." And this was true.

Can you imagine waking up one day with no idea where you are, wearing clothes you'd never wear, answering to a name that isn't yours? Neither could I, but that's what happened to me. I've told essentially no one this story, because frankly it sounds like a world of bullshit, and if someone told me the same thing I'd tell them as much.

I had experienced the psychiatrically rare *psychogenic fugue state.*

What a state it was.

From Wikipedia, one of my favorite websites:

> *Dissociative fugue, formerly fugue state or psychogenic fugue, is a dissociative disorder.[1] It is a rare psychiatric disorder characterized by amnesia for personal identity, including the memories, personality, and other identifying characteristics*

of individuality. The state can last days, months or longer. Dissociative fugue usually involves unplanned travel or wandering, and is sometimes accompanied by the establishment of a new identity. It is a facet of dissociative amnesia, according to the fifth edition of the Diagnostic and Statistical Manual of Mental Disorders (DSM-5).

And: Fugues are precipitated by a series of long-term traumatic episodes.

Check, and check. The first part describes my two months on the run from myself. The last sentence describes the acute period that preceded my vanishing, as well as more generally, the previous twenty-two years of my life. But I don't mean to sound like I'm complaining. I'm certain by now I've caused an equivalent amount of harm in the world during the second half of my life to counterbalance the harm caused to me in the first.

I will often tell people that my forty-first birthday was the day when more American veterans of the Vietnam war died by suicide than during the actual conflict. This is a complete lie, although that day *has* come and gone. I'm uncertain why I tell this story, except that maybe I hope buried deep within such a heavy, albeit fabricated moment, lies some metaphor that may explain what it is that I feel inside me, but is not *of* me, and should be excised. Which is to say, I understand when people shake their heads and tell me that there's simply no way I could lose two months of my life.

One day I woke up in a small room. Nothing in it was familiar. Or rather, everything within it was remarkably *unfamiliar*. Across from my bed a modest crucifix hung on an otherwise empty wall. I felt paralyzed by unknowingness. I had no idea how I'd ended up in this room, and more urgently, why I'd gone to sleep in a pair of acid-washed jeans. In 1996 acid-washed jeans were only seen on the bodies of dads attempting to be hip, Southern spree killers, people in comas, and the occasional over-burdened foster mother whose collection of children reminded one of the eccentric cat collector, making you worry for those under her watch, rather than give thanks that some people are just so very generous with their time and space. When I went to take a piss in the water-closet, something I'd only ever heard existed, I was wearing Y-front underwear, which I hadn't worn since I was a child. My hair was brushed, which I'd never done before and haven't done since. Next to the bed I saw a stack of paperback books, all by John Grisham. I don't want to come across as pompous, but I'd never read a John Grisham book before; those were the type of fluffy books my mother read. I thought this at twenty-two. At forty-three I have no problem with fluffy books, and often wish I had the ability to write one, as they seem to be quite lucrative. At the time though I'd been obsessed with Vladimir Nabokov, Martin Amis, Philip Roth, Saul Bellow. All the writers you'd check off when describing the cliché of a nascent, white, male intellectual.

I felt like someone from a sci-fi movie who'd been put into cryostasis only to awaken fifty years later, except that I didn't remember my mission. I felt like the protagonist of every epi-sode of The Twilight Zone. I had no choice but to leave my room and see what world I was in. I opened my door and found there was nowhere to go but down the flight of stairs leading up to it. As soon as my nose entered the ground floor, I began to hear "Good morning Peter." Who the fuck was Peter? I'd always hated my name, Brad, but Peter was no improvement. If I'd planned on starting my life over, done some witness protection thing, I think I would have gone with Edmund or Walter, some-thing CIA Director sounding. Not Peter. Peter is the guy who does everything and the guy who does nothing. Peter is your sis-ter's husband, Peter is the neighbor who wants to "catch a beer",

Peter is your waiter at IHOP, Peter is working on his "mancave." Why would I be Peter?

My experience in the coffee shop I'd walked into (apparently, I'd been renting a room directly above it) was extraordinarily rattling, and I had to do my very best to stifle a scream, pretending I knew these people who obviously knew me. I said a singular "Good Morning" to cover everyone, then went to sit at an empty table. A matronly woman asked me what was wrong. What *was* wrong?

"Peter, you're so silly. Go sit at your table. I'm warming up the cherry pie right now."

I walked towards the corner table I'd seen her glance at, and sat in what felt like a bucket of warm light. I did like cherry pie, as Brad. Apparently certain things had carried over. I detested coffee though, which was what accompanied the pie that arrived instantly.

"What book are you on now?" the matronly woman asked with what I found to be disturbingly genuine interest. Disturbing also was that she lingered at my table after bringing my breakfast. The place was deserted. I'd only seen waitresses do this in films with characters who were long-standing regulars, lonely types who treated people in the service industry as de facto psychologists.

I followed her eyes to my hand, and realized I'd brought with me a copy, dog-eared about halfway through, of John Grisham's legal thriller, *The Chamber.*

"*The Chamber,*" I heard myself say. I saw her watching my mouth to see what words I'd form next, so tried out "How was your evening?" She was about to take a seat and begin actually answering me when three truck drivers walked the through the front door, prompting her to rise and greet them with small town geniality. She touched my shoulder warmly as she departed.

I was disturbed most by my outfit. Around this time I listened to a lot of Fugazi, as did my friends. We were all into

Washington/Arlington scene stuff, Nation of Ulysses and Drag City low-fi sad-sacks, interchangeable post-punk hardcore bands (I'm embarrassed to write these words) and a great deal of free jazz. As a result we all wore Dickie's, plain t-shirts with no logos, short-sleeved plaid shirts, and plain shoes of one type or another. This acid-wash was really fucking with my head, as was, what I slowly came to notice, the cable-knit white Tommy Hilfiger sweater I was wearing, the collars of a baby-blue dress shirt bothering my neck and throat. Tommy Hilfiger, of the massive cocaine empire which funded a massive fashion empire which was then co-opted by hip-hop culture which trickled down to street-level to be reincorporated back into a cocaine empire. Also though, bullshit worn by people who liked to sail and have children who speak French.

I ate the cherry pie because no matter what had happened I wasn't an idiot. Then a girl came over to my table, someone that in my head I thought was named Julie (the only partial memory I retained from my dissociative vacation), but knew nothing more about. Julie was cute, I could have tried to keep it together for a bit in the hopes of getting Julie's sweater off back in my bedroom, but I was quickly becoming undone.

Then it happened. I heard myself scream at the top of my lungs, "Where the fuck am I, and who the fuck are you people?"

Everyone in the coffee shop looked disappointedly at me. An elderly man audibly hissed while glancing at me over his reading glasses.

I felt it as it happened, my hand slowly releasing the legal thriller I had no memory of getting two-hundred odd pages into, aware in slow-motion I'd never find out how it ended, while also aware I had no idea how it began. I fell from my chair, sideways, landing on the floor. The last sound I heard was the deep, nauseating crack of my cheekbone against unforgiving hardwood.

Forty-eight hours later I came to in a hospital in Peterborough, two hours by car from Toronto where I'd lived all my life.

Peterborough, where I'd never been before and had no reason to be now.

As I came out of my slumber a small group of doctors surrounded me, all with clipboards in their hands.

"So, Peter, can you tell us what you remember?" one of them asked.

"I don't know who Peter is. I don't know who you are. I don't know why I'm here. I don't wear acid-washed clothing. I don't understand any of this. I want to get out of here. I hate all you motherfu-"

I felt the effect of the needle before I felt it pierce my skin, and it was another two days before I would be awake again.

I was fully Brad again, which was a disappointment. A team of doctors explained to me what a psychogenic fugue state was. I explained the flurry of trauma I'd experienced before the 'event', and they said this was completely normal, symptomatically accurate, it's a lot for one person to absorb Brad. All of them 'you poor-thinged' me, which I enjoyed. I was told those two months would never return to me, and was warned against trying to recover memories of my lost time via hypnosis, LSD, tantric sex or any other method I might feel tempted to employ.

My girlfriend showed up in her Nissan Altima. When I got in the passenger seat she gave me a cigarette. I realized I hadn't smoked while I was in the hospital, and apparently not at all during my two-month David Copperfielding, as I got a wicked head rush. We listened to Jawbreaker on tape and made the two-hour drive back in silence. Occasionally Yasmin would put her hand on my shoulder, but that was it. She appeared to be slightly scared of me, and I felt that was appropriate.

I didn't tell anyone what had happened to me, including my

mother. Only Yasmin knew. For my mother, I concocted a lie about riding the rails to Chicago with my friends to go see Archie Shepp play a show with Jeanne Lee. "Really, you should have let someone know", she said. I told her she was right and I was sorry. She said sometimes I was just like my father, but did not say "may he rest in peace."

Six years later I moved to Vancouver. I have only a handful of memories between the years 2008-10, but this is a different sort of amnesia; self-induced. I was suicidal but lazy so was going the route of hepatitis or cirrhosis or accidental overdose or HIV in a blackout. One of my few memories of that time was asking Diego from whom I often scored dope to get me a gun. I had the money, he knew that much. He asked me what I wanted it for, and I said revenge, trying to appeal to his mentality. He asked me revenge against who, and I mistakenly said myself, giving away that I wanted to end my life. He said, "Hey man, no way," his vowels stretching into whale music. I asked him why he was so moral suddenly, since he sold me dope daily that was killing me, but wouldn't sell me a gun that would kill me instantly.

"I'm Catholic," was his response, pointing to the tattoo of a crucifix on his chest, obscured by a giant gold crucifix worn around his neck. I asked him what he meant, but before he could offer me any rational response I realized I had a flap in my hand, and was slowly walking back to where I lived, a place I cannot remember now. Then I heard him yell behind me,

"It's also just bad business B!"

Now it is the present. I am forty-three years old, and married to a gifted, beautiful, Miami-born artist and writer named Cristine Salcedo, whom I met online while she was living in China and I was living in a basement suite, miserable and alone, churning out watercolour paintings to avoid going to twelve-step meetings. Avoiding going to twelve-step meetings because at those meeting I'd be told that doing drugs was a bad idea. It worked for me, and to this day I am, to use the hygienically stigmatizing language of recovery culture, still "clean." All throughout my time in Vancouver, and for the last five years that I've been back home in Toronto, I've had a constant, low-grade anxiety about running into someone who knew me as Peter. It's not a fear that comes up daily, but it's there. I've never forgotten how the doctors in Peterborough made it sound like any interaction, physical or conceptual with those two months of lost time, could cause me untold harm and psychic trauma. It often felt like that cliché from films about time travel. Never ever fuck with the past, don't even move a hat on a bed half an inch, because you could cause a sequence of events that might lead, quite melodramatically in my opinion, to the end of life on Earth as we know it.

Two months ago, I turned in the completed manuscript of my first collection of short stories, *Essays and Fictions*, to my publisher Giancarlo DiTrapano, of Tyrant Books. I started to write fiction in rehab, and found it much more challenging and satisfying than painting felt at that point. Two months ago I also had a chunk of money fall into my Dickie's clad lap. Gian had extended me an open invitation, during the writing of the book or basically whenever I wanted, to come with my wife to his family's estate south of Rome and stay for free. I'd only have to pay the cleaning fee. I knew that if I went there intending to write, Cristine and I would be too distracted by the beauty of the environment (never mind the outdoor pool with a view of the Mediterranean), to get any real work done. So, I decided to wait until my manuscript was complete. My agent, who'd just begun shaving, had signed off on it, full of enthusiasm, and Gian was also convinced this book might really get people's attention. Being new to writing, and thinking most of my stories were too sexually disgusting to reach a wide audience, I appreciated their support, but wasn't going to quit my day job. My day job being making art and receiving disability benefits.

The galleys would be printed by the time Cristine and I left Italy to return to Toronto. We decided we'd stay at Gian's place for a month. He was sending excerpts to the Paris Review, my agent to the New Yorker. Both felt far out of my league, but then I realized that leagues no longer existed. The only leagues were "new", and the senior's league, the softball league called "old." Cristine reminded me that the Paris Review *had* given my short novella about doing massive amounts of drugs and ruining my life critic's pick on their website after Gian sent the editor a copy, but that seemed fluky to me, the book having been described as "not exactly edifying", which, with my tendency to see clouds bereft of silver and full of dog shit, led me to somehow forget the rest of the brief write-up, which actually said many nice things about what I wrote and how I wrote it.

I prayed about my poor self-image infecting my sense of what this book may do. I prayed for those people much smarter than I who were now in control of what I wrote. I prayed often and regularly. And then, with Cristine having turned in her own manuscript for a chapbook of poems, we took a taxi to the airport, watched twenty-seven episodes of Frasier in diaper redolent coach, and emerged with our bags into the art historical pornography of Rome.

However, since both of us had no interest in this pornography, we grabbed some food and headed immediately to the train station.

The ride to Sezze was brief, and the countryside was beautiful. When we got off the train there was no sign of Giancarlo, who texted to say he was running a bit late. We decided to eat gelato and sit in the sun. At this point it would be normal I suppose to provide descriptive passages of the landscape, the quaintness of this small village. I could offer a detailed description of an old Italian widow, clad in black, her face weathered from a lifetime of Catholic self-abnegation and good honest work, carrying a basket of fresh something as she walked slowly up a cobblestone hill, her cane and old-fashioned peasant determination propelling her forward, if slowly. But why. We've all seen the photos, the movies, the postcards, the independent films. It looked exactly as Italy should, and there's really no point in going on much more about it. I could just as simply describe what my left hand looked like holding a cigarette, but again, we all know about hands.

Getting bored, we heard a car horn blast three times, and the sound of someone yelling my name.

"Brad!" was what we heard.

Turning toward the noise, there was Giancarlo, impeccably styled, seemingly always just out of bed, standing next to a gleaming white, vintage Porsche Carrera. As we approached each other Cristine remarked smartly that there was just no fucking room for our luggage in this little hitman of a car. After hugging and kissing and basically acting European, Cristine and I got into the tiny back seat, each of us with our carry-on bags in our laps. Gian had put the large suitcase on top of the car, unsecured by anything other than his left hand. He drove not slowly out of the village and up a winding hill, cigarette in his mouth, looking back to speak to us both. Cristine and I mentally communicated a sense of disbelief that he could do all of this this while keeping our heavy suitcase on top of the car with only the strength of his arm.

We were both speechless once we arrived at where we'd been assured we could stay for free. I briefly considered that Giancarlo was insane or perhaps had confused my manuscript with someone else's. That first evening was lovely, and I could describe the meal, the conversation, the atmosphere, the walk through the olive grove. But it would sound just as you'd expect it to. I don't drink at all and Cristine very little, so Gian and his husband Giuseppe took their alcohol cups and walked towards the main house. A romantic couple, vanishing arm in arm, swallowed by the night's end. Cristine and I were exhausted, and after taking off our clothes and getting into bed (the small house we were staying in was beautiful and could also be described at length) we were both asleep before we'd had a chance to say a word to each other about the evening. In the morning I woke up with my mouth pressed against my wife's, as if we'd drifted off while kissing each other goodnight. I thought it was very beautiful. Almost every morning, I get up before Cristine, and in our apartment in Philadelphia, due to when I wake up and the angle of the fabric covering our bedroom window, her face is often rendered sculptural by a swath of golden light. I have an annoying tendency to photograph her while she sleeps, the light emphasizing her bone structure in innumerable ways I find painfully beautiful. I am scared to turn the sound of the camera down on my phone, fearing it will stop my alarm from ringing, something Cristine has told me repeatedly will not happen, so she'll often wake up thanks to the accurate shutter sound of my phone to find me on my knees in the bed next to her, photographing her face, her nose, her hair.

That morning though I just stared. A lot had happened to me in eight years, and a lot had happened to us in three. I'd once had a fairly good shot at being an artist of real success who might have found himself staying for free in some absurdly luxurious European hideaway. But I burned all of that to the ground. That I'd been able to attain an equivalent experience utilizing a skill I'd been embarrassed to try out, at a time when I was no longer a slave to drugs and alcohol, and had the privilege of loving and being loved by a woman who restored my faith in all things in which faith can be restored, well, it made me forget my phone and taking photographs. I can resolutely say that that first morning in Sezze, I had never felt so grateful in my life, never so lucky, and never so determined to not let anything fuck with the small paradise that was my daily experience as a middle-aged man who surely did not deserve the life he was living.

We spent the next day exploring the property. We swam in the pool. We had sex under a tree that must have been at least ten thousand years old.. Gian and Giuseppe gave us our privacy, which was unnecessary but kind. For the first time in what seemed like two years to us, Cristine and I could breathe. We were not worrying about the future or entangled in the past. We'd each worked hard, had things upcoming to show for it, and let ourselves, as people with compromised self-esteem, truly believe that we deserved this vacation. In the evening, she read to me from a book of Philip Larkin poems. Later she made me laugh uncontrollably describing her future plan to establish a film production company which only distributed films "made *by* pigs, *for* pigs." Some of the titles were unbelievably funny. Any capital letters she described as being "key", creatively. *CORN ON THE COB, again.* This was her first film. It had something to do with pigs being sick and tired of corn on the cob. *9 SECONDS OF BOOTY* made you think it was porcine-porno but was actually a Western, and *OINKERS* was a film about the counter-intelligence community. It was so quiet where we were, quieter than any place I'd been in a long time, that I imagined weary villagers annoyed at my hysterically asking Cristine to explain the plot of *OINKERS* again, particularly the scene where a Russian pig spy has difficulty attaching his fake mustache with spirit glue using only his hooves and a strong sense of patriotism.

On our second morning I woke up just before sunrise, probably due to jet-lag. Cristine looked like a painting of Sappho while she slept, and I figured I should let her enjoy what she was doing, as she often has trouble sleeping. I considered going back to bed but instead thought I'd explore the early morning. I hadn't been awake at this time since before I got sober, and back then it would have been because I hadn't slept yet, or wasn't sleeping at all. I smoked a cigarette on the porch, wrapped in a blanket, then wrote Cristine a note to say I was up and going to look around, not to worry. I put on my clothes, got on one of the rickety twelve-speeds that was leaning up against the house, and set off towards the small center of town, figuring I could recreate some scene from an early 20th century novel I may or may not have read, where the husband returns with a loaf of bread still warm from the bakery, some olives, cheese and eggs, and makes his wife breakfast while she talks to him from bed, a sheet wrapped loosely around her body.

The light was beautiful as the sun floated up. It was lovely to hear only the sounds of birds and of other animals I didn't recognize. I don't know if Italy has foxes, but I imagined very clearly an image of the classic Italian Wood Fox. I mostly rode the bike in lazy circles for a while. It was nice to be back on one, another thing I hadn't done in a very long time. I saw an old man in the distance, or rather I saw the generative puffs of smoke involved in starting a pipe. I figured that another residence must mean that was the way towards the markets and cappuccino joints and lace makers and whatever other Italianesque shit went down in Sezze. When I passed the old man on my bicycle I stupidly smiled at him like Jude Law from some late Woody Allen movie, and he just spit some tobacco out of his mouth, basically right at me. I felt invigorated and humiliated at once.

Eventually I realized I was on a trail, and felt what I thought was far too much of a sense of accomplishment. I hadn't split the atom, I'd just figured out the way to town. As I got closer the trail became less haphazard, and small houses began to appear. They all looked exactly as you'd think they should. Maybe women were putting clothes out to dry, I have no idea. I was mostly inside of my idea of what a small Italian town should be, not actively observing what it was. Then I heard a car honk, a Euro honk, and a small, slowly awakening commercial enclave appeared before me. I rode into it, trying to "soak up the atmosphere" or something like that. I leaned my bicycle against a pole outside of maybe a cheese shop and stood there, smoking a cigarette and looking at what felt mostly like a scene from film, which led me to think about how much I hated postmodernism.

I could see people staring at me, and this felt right. It made me uncomfortable and this also felt right. This would be the price I'd pay for getting to have such a precious experience for free. Everything was as it should have been. I came out of the bakery with the warm, absurdly long loaf of bread under my arm. Although I detest coffee, for some reason I felt it was imperative that I sit at one of two cafes and have a cappuccino. "Un cappuc-cino per piacere," I think I said, which I'm embarrassed to admit, as I realize now I should have used "favore" instead. I sipped the disgusting beverage, wondering where the tall, fresh-faced, beau-tiful Italian women were, out doing their shopping, about to run into their future husbands. Then I asked myself what the fuck made me think that was a thing? That I'd see that? The other café was pretty much just across the cobblestone street from the one I was sitting at, and I saw two couples, obviously also not locals, sauntering slowly towards it, their body language indicating a night involving too much wine. They were unremarkable. Two couples, each male and female. One of the couples looked to be around my age, in their mid-forties. The other couple was comprised of a man maybe my age with a woman perhaps a decade younger. A couple like Cristine and I. I didn't care much for their style. The man with the younger woman literally had only the bottom button of his shirt connected, which I thought absolutely repugnant. All four were wearing flip-flops, another unforgivable transgression. I didn't pay much attention to the women but found myself focusing on the man with the younger partner. Why would he do that with his shirt? Why would she find that attractive? I decided I didn't care, put money down for my cappuccino, crossed the street, and went to find olives and eggs for Cristine.

When I walked past the foursome, the man with the button-less shirt looked me in the eyes slightly longer than I considered appropriate. Not that this is a thing that makes me want to fight or anything like with some men, I just didn't like it. Once past them I saw that if I made a left I'd hit what seemed to be the olive district.

I turned the corner, leaving the couples behind, along with the memory of my cappucino (assisted in doing so by smoking another cigarette), when I heard rushing footsteps behind me.

"Peter?" was what I heard. The voice sounded North American.

I kept walking. Maybe they were talking to someone else.

"Peter!" came the sound again.

Understand that while I've said I always live with a low-grade anxiety about my fugue state, it doesn't mean that every time I hear the name Peter I get terrified of finding out something about my two months away. A lot of people are named Peter, part of why I hated that I'd chosen that name for myself.

Then I felt a hand on my shoulder, which I really did not appreciate. I spun around. It was the man who could not button his shirt.

"Peter. It's me, Kevin. Kevin Taylor. I know it's been a long time but c'mon man, we hung out every day twenty years ago. Then one day you were just gone. What happened to you anyway?"

I realized that it was all happening right now, in the most unlikely place, so remote, so secluded. This was information from the past I must not hear lest it cause me psychic trauma or instigate a new narrative in my life that could involve radical alterations I was not interested in. So, I did this:

"Oh, hey buddy. Kevin. Good to see you man, weird place to see you man."

"I *know*, right? So, *beautiful* here, right? What are you *doing* here?"

I knew I couldn't let the conversation go on much longer in case he told me something I shouldn't know. I already felt a squirming revulsion at myself for having spent "every day" with the kind of guy that would only button the bottom of his shirt, leaving his chest to assault passerby. Maybe this information alone was starting to change my life? I began to panic. I didn't understand, this was over twenty years later. I had a beard now, half grey. At twenty-two I had no beard. I had fourteen teeth in my face now, at twenty-two I had all but three. I was covered in tattoos now, at twenty-two I had only a handful. More importantly and most confusedly, the way I'd lived made it appear as if I'd put my face through a carwash run on cat shit, glass, and suede shoe spray hundreds of times. I did not resemble the person I'd been then. I did not understand how he could recognize me.

Then, for some reason, I thought of Patricia Highsmith. I thought of the three essays I'd written in the last two years, each of them desperate to get people to pay attention to her work. To take her more seriously. If I did this, it wouldn't help, but it would indicate an even more serious commitment to championing her work, even if that made no sense and in fact would result in nothing of the sort.

"Listen man," I said, "why don't you walk to this olive joint with me and we can catch up. I'm sorta in a rush, my wife is pregnant and just waking up probably very hungry back at the place we're staying at."

"Sure man" said Kevin, just as someone named Kevin would. "Sure man."

I managed to buy some olives quickly with Kevin, who kept peppering me with questions but thankfully hadn't told me anything about what happened in 1996 yet. It was not a bustling olive district, it was two shops that sold olives, and a bunch of other businesses that were either not yet open or abandoned. I told Kevin I needed to take a piss, and we walked to what was the dead end of the small street. Thankfully, and almost right from one of her books, "Kev" said he also had to piss. So as not to insult the locals, we walked past the end of the street and up a small incline, into a slightly forested area that the sun hadn't yet infiltrated. I did not remove anything from my pants as I had no need to piss. But while Kevin faced a tree, some Italian type I'd never seen before, I waited until I saw him shift his weight, indicating he'd pulled his dick out. I listened for the trickle. He was still trying to talk to me but I only heard mumbling. There were many to choose from, but the largest rock I felt I could lift was right at my feet. I put the bread down, raised the almost-boulder with surprising ease, and while Kevin began to say "Hey, do you remember that girl-", I lifted the rock far over my head, bringing it down with all my strength and the kindness of gravity onto the top of his head. I heard a rather unsettling crack, and felt something not liquid, not solid, hit me in the forehead. Kevin went down immediately, and it was obvious that he was as dead as he'd ever be. His head had split in half quite cartoonishly. I thought I saw steam coming off his brain and wondered if brains are hot.

Strangely, like Tom Ripley himself, I felt nothing. No panic, no remorse. I was wholly present, and I liked the parallels. I myself abhor violence, but letting myself occupy a character from fiction, especially to protect an unknown fictionalized version of myself that had once truly existed, somehow it all felt okay. I couldn't let Kevin ruin my life. I couldn't run the risk of learning about those two months.

I'd thought while I walked with him towards the olive shop that I was doing a scene from *The Talented Mr. Ripley*, that I would assume Kevin's identity, somehow receive money from his parents; that basically I would now impersonate him for the rest of my life. But then I remembered Cristine, and I also remembered the girl Kevin was with, the type of girl who could date a man who buttoned his shirt in such an unseemly way. So, it wasn't that book I was re-enacting.

I realized as I hid his body under branches and wiped pieces of brain off my sweater and face, that really, with my deep knowledge of Patricia Highsmith's body of work, my rereading of everything she ever wrote multiple times, that what I had done could more accurately be described as the performance of a Highsmithian narrative. The one it resembled most was definitely a Tom Ripley narrative, but she'd written other characters I could also see this situation belonging to.

I felt hungry. I worried that I'd been gone too long and Cristine might be lonely, or wondering if I was okay. Walking back towards my bike I saw one of the couples alone, and realized that the younger woman must be off panicked, looking for Kevin. I felt nothing about it, other than that I'd had no choice.

Everything in the town looked as it should. It was now early morning. The cafes were full, the shops busy. Everyone was dressed as you'd expect them to be, and the black-clad widows dotted the crowd. I got back on my bike, giant loaf of bread under my shoulder, having forgotten the eggs, and steered with my right hand, my left one holding a small container of what I hoped Cristine would think were very classy olives.

BOO-HOO IN THREE PARTS

I have a story to tell.

Here it comes.

1.

Maybe 1996

September 1st, 1996 my father died. (*The young man got off the subway at St. Clair West station, the Heath Street exit. It's a beautiful exit, a very rarefied area of Toronto. You can hear the trickling of the ravine, see joggers. He lit a cigarette while he was climbing the stairs to exit the station. It was two in the afternoon and there weren't many people around. It felt like autumn although it was still technically summer; the leaves were already various oranges and reds. The air felt sharp against the soft skin of his neck. He walked west towards Bathurst Street as he had done so many times before. He passed the tree in the park across the street on which someone had wrapped different colored scarves around the ornate branches. Over the last year the scarves had become more weathered and muted. He was getting excited to get where he was going, to do what he was going to do. The feeling never lost its intensity during this ritual. At Bathurst, he pressed the button for the crosswalk. The light could never change quickly enough. Crossing the street he passed the store, Sun Variety, where he would later, during these trips, go slowly and with lethargic movements, if he could, to buy cigarettes and ginger ale. He walked north on Bathurst, past Claxton street, past the strangely out of place Tudor house that was gated off with no discernible entrance, containing obscure and what seemed like geographically inappropriate trees in various states of decomposition. Left on Claxton, a park was a few blocks away where sometimes they would go and, out of their minds, attempt to watch West Indian men play cricket while their wives and children cooked. Two walk-ups in he arrived at the building. He put his key in the door and did the irritating wiggle that sometimes took time to unlock the knob. He smelled the smell, he thought of how all buildings and houses had their own unique smells. He walked up the threadbare burgundy carpeted steps to the third floor, to apartment 303. He knocked and waited. After ten seconds he knocked again, but he wasn't let in. This wasn't unusual, so he used the key he had for the apartment and let himself in. The room smelled like it usually did, of stale American cigarettes and alcohol. The marbled cat came at him quickly, and looked at him in a way he hadn't seen before. The young man walked into the kitchen, called out the name and heard no reply. This again was not unusual. He made himself a drink and while doing so noticed the cat directing him to its empty bowls of food and water. He fed the cat. He walked out of the kitchen and into the living room. Then he saw it. His father was sitting on the sofa he always sat in, naked, with a needle angling precariously from the inside of his elbow. His eyes were wide open, staring off at some point between the floor and the ceiling, as if transfixed by a beautiful painting. It was obvious that he was dead. He was grey, or greyer than usual. The young man was not entirely surprised by the reality of this situation; there welled up inside of him a brief moment of sorrow, maybe shock—and then immediately his eyes fixed upon the flaps of heroin sitting on the coffee table. He took a Camel out of a pack sitting on the table and lit it. The cat jumped up into his arms and he stayed there holding it, looking at his unmoving father and smoking until the cigarette was finished, ashing on the floor, which he wouldn't have ordinarily done. Certain things passed through his mind, obvious things and complex things. Emotions came and went as quickly as the sound of cars passing you on the highway. He was trying to make a decision. Looking again at the dope on the table, the answer came quickly. He put down the cat, and went to sit next to his father on the couch. His face was cold to the touch.*

His father had known he was coming, they'd spoken only three hours before, so he knew that things would not, according at least to what popular culture had told him, start to smell unpleasant for a while. He examined his father's dead face and thought of his own, how similar they were, how they both looked much older than they were. There was piss between his father's legs on the grey velour couch; he reached over for a blanket and put it across his lap. The realization that had come so quickly to him was this: coroners are not in a hurry to catalogue the dead, but police officers are in a hurry to confiscate narcotics. So with that in my mind, he began to empty the flaps onto the coffee table, took a fresh sheet of foil from the roll on the floor, took out his lighter, and began the beloved ritual. The Three Stooges were on the television, what would turn out to be a marathon. Months ago the volume had broken, so he liked that it was a show you could enjoy without sound. The Three Stooges were also something they'd enjoyed together when he was a child. His father had a greasy glass pipe on the table next to four empty packs of cigarettes, a bottle of Jim Beam that had a fair amount left in it, and a yellowed Polaroid of a naked girl, one leg tied to a radiator, smiling and giving the thumbs up, with a cigarette dangling from her swollen bottom lip. He measured out a point of smack on a folded sheet of foil and attached a clip. He held it under his chin, held the lighter underneath, waited for the smoke to develop, then sucked all of it in with his father's pipe. He had time to put the pipe on the table and drop the foil before slowly sinking back into the couch, his head at a similarly dead angle as his father's. Very slowly, he started to lean sideways, until he found his head resting against the cold shoulder of the corpse. None of this struck him as unusual. He focused his eyes on Larry hitting Curly in the head repeatedly with a two by four. No clocks, no watches; time does not inhabit these experiences. He was made alert by a sound. A slow, bizarre octave that was coming somewhere from his father's body. Gas or air. There was no way to locate the suddenly activated orifice, no smell or audible clue as to what was happening. Then it stopped. He took his head off the dead shoulder and sat upright, looking over. His father was quite beautiful in a broken, cadavular way. Something about death had made the paleness of his blue eyes paler, as if the color was leaking out. He didn't want to close them with his fingers as he'd seen on TV because he wanted to feel like they were looking at each other. He put another cigarette in his mouth and lit it, and the cat came and lay near his feet. He touched his father's white hair, and then a fly landed on his cheek. He watched the fly clean its wings and stroked his father's hair. There would be more bugs, some inside and some coming to nest. More worrisome were the ones inside.

People say it's impossible to die in your dreams. The young man often dreamt of his death. The night before he came to party with his father, he dreamt that he was waiting for the bus. He craned his neck out too far, the bus was suddenly there, and the side mirror clipped his head clean off. His rolling head was still conscious and observed the sky then the concrete then a flash of faces then a tanning salon. He had dreamt of being shot, stabbed, drowned, buried alive. After each of these dreams, waking up, the first thing he felt was disappointment. Each day upon waking the thought that popped into his mind first was "Fuck, here we go again." So, to see his father finally having been allowed to vacate the jumble of organs receiving constant signals from an antagonistic brain, he felt that his father was lucky.

He was in a way surprised and then not, at how comfortable he was sitting next to the corpse. Sitting next to his dad, the corpse. He kept on smoking the dope, petting the cat, watching Mo chase Larry with a hammer, watching Curly and Mo push a heavy matronly type back and forth in an gaudily decorated pantry. He had found in a bathroom drawer a carton of Camel Lights, and there was another bottle of bourbon in the bathtub. He had no reason to leave, didn't want to, and felt perfectly at home. It was the only chance he'd ever had to inspect the environment his father spent all his time in.

He found no photographs, letters or ephemera related to their being son and father. This didn't surprise him. He did find, in a sort of shamefully hidden corner of the bedroom, evidence of his father's obsession with Luther Vandross. Every album, seven inch, posters, ticket stubs. He kept stumbling on strange photographs of young, bruised girls bound to things: chairs, beds, hogtied in closets. Always smiling though, and for some reason very often giving the classic thumbs up. He could tell some of the Polaroids had been taken in this very apartment. Some were obviously in hotels. He had never been aware of his dad having any interest in deviant sexuality, and with his deep knowledge of smack, he knew how very uninteresting sex could become to the professional junky. So the Polaroids were slightly confusing. There were about a dozen, never the same girl twice: one Native girl, one black girl, the rest very similar-looking scrawny white girls in their late twenties or early thirties, all with similarly small breasts, oddly placed bruises, scratches, fat lips, traces of fading black eyes. There was something reassuring about how happy they all looked though. He noticed a crepuscular shift in the room, shadows vanishing; he thought about turning on a light then decided against it. He took out a cigarette, put it between his dad's lips, lit it, smoked a rather gigantic point, then lay his head on the dead lap. He smoked his own cigarette with difficulty, and the ashes fell onto his shirt. The ashes from his father's unpuffable cigarette landed on his forehead. He felt the urine that had soaked into the blanket start to dampen his hair. It was sort of beautiful, a physical closeness they'd never shared before. The cat climbed up on the couch and lay between the young man's legs. He felt loved. He started to see different images in the stucco ceiling. It reminded him of games he would play with his father at the cottage in the late 70's, picking shapes out of clouds. He had sort of drifted off, then was awakened by a strange jolt his father's leg made. And then came a long, slow, gaseous moan. He sat back up and looked at his face. He was definitely dead, no getting around it, not a dream. The cigarette he'd given him had burnt down to the end and left a red mark on his bottom lip. He looked hard into the unseeing eyes. There was nothing there, but that in a way was not new. What was new was that his father had an excuse for such vacancy and indifference now. He guessed the body did strange things after death, sometimes muscles pop or contract. The sound had not made a smell. He supposed slowly gases were finding points of escape. Probably it was the middle of the night. He couldn't see much but what the moon illuminated. The light on the table thankfully disclosed a coffee mug, the bourbon, another sizable pile of smack and the pipe. He filled the coffee cup up with Jim Beam, drank it all down in two gulps, sucked up one more giant point, then lay on his side with his legs tucked up and fell asleep with his face pressed against his father's belly. The oppressive horror of the sun woke him up the next day. He put his hand over his eyes and fished a cigarette by feel off the table and into his mouth, lit it and thought a bit. He heard the cat crying somewhere in the apartment. He realized this was the longest period of time he'd spent with his father in almost fifteen years. He sat up slowly, drank some bourbon from the bottle, and looked at the body. His father's face had changed in a way he couldn't really understand. He looked more dead he supposed. His father's head was now slumped at an impossible angle against his shoulder, he imagined the result of rigor mortis wearing off. The head was in a position that implied a broken neck. He slowly became conscious of quite a bad smell. It was coming from between his dad's legs. Death had slowly facilitated the release of the fugitive and difficult junky bowel movement. Again, this all felt natural. He wasn't disturbed or upset. He got up off the couch with the slow, deliberate movements of a modern dancer. The cat followed him into the bathroom and watched him piss in the sink. There was no mirror, and he realized that there had never been any mirrors in this apartment. Mirrors are emissaries of unwanted consciences, so his father had dispatched them from his life. He started smoking another cigarette and fed the cat, who was quite beautiful in the sun of whatever time of day it was. He looked in the refrigerator, rather naively he realized, and of course there was nothing but an old squeeze container of Dijon mustard, Chinese take-out boxes that were likely from another year, and for some reason a cellular telephone. The hunger pain was brief and vanished, and probably not even genuine, just the mind giving him advice. The cat jumped into his arms, and he held it while he smoked and went back to staring at his father. He had never looked deader, more corpse-like. He knew this made sense since he actually was dead now. The needle was still hanging off his arm acrobatically, like a stripper with powerful legs frozen on a pole in a placement that defied gravity. 'Do organs contain memories?' flashed into his head. If he took a knife from the kitchen, carved out his father's kidney and ate it, would he know what was behind those Polaroids? Would he have a better understanding of what his father thought of him? The smell was troublesome. There were more than a few flies resting in and around his father's face now. He watched them trying to make their way under the blanket he had draped over his lap. He dragged a piece of shit chair from the kitchen over to the table while holding the cat, sat down opposite the body and kept looking. The eyes were looking at him, but through him. And again, this was not something death had made unique. He'd received this look innumerable times. He'd also given it. He realized there was only one more sizable point of dope left on the table. He slowly gathered it together on the foil with a card and put the cat down. He drank more bourbon from the bottle. He removed the cigarette butt that had left the burn mark on his father's lip. He felt stupid about that, as if he had desecrated a corpse. There was no reason to have done it and he felt guilty and juvenile. He smoked the last of the heroin. It wasn't enough to really get him high, not as high as he wanted to be. He didn't know what time it was and that was fine. He polished off the remaining Jim Beam. He found a plastic Loblaws bag next to the couch and put what remained of the carton of cigarettes inside of it. He took the Polaroids. He went up close to his father, ran his fingers through his thin grey hair. He kissed him on the lips, keeping them there for what felt like a long time. He stood back and smoked and

looked hard at his Dad, to fix the moment in his mind. Not as a reminder to stop the way he was living, that wasn't even on the radar. He just wanted to hold this image in his mind forever, of his father staring at and through him, his head angled so strangely, the light throwing shadows into the pockets of his face. He left his keys to the apartment on the table. He picked up the cat and whispered sweet nothings in its ear, then held it down on the floor of the kitchen with a washcloth over its head and pulverized its skull with one solid blow from a heavy steel knife sharpener he'd found. He did not look back. He didn't have any emotions about the last twenty-four (if they were) hours. Perhaps there was a moment of gratitude for this last bit of time he was able to spend with his father. More so, he felt grateful for all that available dope. He walked down the stairs of the building for the last time, was attacked by the sun, turned right on Bathurst past the anachronistic Tudor house to the Shell station, where he picked up the greasy handle of the payphone to call 911.)
The phone rang, and I started to make disturbingly atavistic sounds as soon as my mother picked it up. I knew what was on the other end. I was only there visiting. I shouldn't have been present for the phone call.

2.

Definitely 2018

I've always been bad at writing in the second person. The third person, which I'm stellar at, doesn't really suit this narrative, so once again Brad Phillips will be the name of a fictional character telling an unpleasant story, and in doing so, Brad Phillips will appear to be more and more of an unpleasant person. This is the risk I'm willing to take for the sake of the writing.

When I was sixteen in 1990, someone close to me gave me a sizable amount of heroin for my birthday. This is where the life I'd been leading up until then, which had mostly been free of drugs but rampant with abuse and shoplifting, came to an end. Once I'd tried out my birthday present, I realized it was either what had been missing my whole life or what would fix my life. At forty-three of course I realize it was neither. At forty-three this knowledge does not mean I don't miss heroin, or am immune from relapsing.

It's Wednesday. Outside my window everything is covered in the first snowfall. I know I will not go outside to smell it and feel it on my face. Monday at 8:30 in the morning, I was at the hospital in the acute stage of opiate withdrawal, to switch to a drug called Suboxone. Suboxone is an opiate, but it's also an opiate babysitter. The main component of the drug (medication) is Buprenorphine: an opioid. The rest of the medication is comprised of Naloxone, the overdose drug that was used on me three? times. As an antagonist it means that were I to consume any other opiate, I wouldn't get high, and the babysitter aspect of the drug would throw me into immediate withdrawal to punish me. It reminds me of the archaic drug Anabuse which I watched my father take and then try to drink through, vomiting blood and seizing.

When I arrived at the hospital my urine smelled Chernoby-lic. I was shivering like an urchin from Dickens. I couldn't stop yawning or tearing up. My legs were on fire, my kidneys felt sore and I was freezing cold, staying inside my parka under a blanket on the hospital bed. The first 4 milligram dose of Sub-oxone immediately put me to sleep. When I woke up two hours later all my withdrawal symptoms were gone. This was much nicer than my rehab experience in 2012, kicking cold turkey in a house full of steelworkers. Then I began to cramp again. The second 4 milligram dose didn't help, nor did the third. I went home with my legs in unbearable pain, and developed a brutal headache.

The next day I returned to the hospital. Before I left, I took my first unlaxativized shit in as long as I can remember. It felt like my asshole had forgotten how to push out excrement. I have not gone to the bathroom again. I wonder if I need to retrain my body, teach it how to shit again. It seems fundamentally wrong to have to learn to shit again. It's a skill that comes at birth. I'm constipated as I type this. My wife Cristine came the second day. I'd cry inexplicably and then stop. I was given 12 milligrams immediately, which made me feel much better. The crying *jags* as people call them continued throughout the day. I was still having withdrawal symptoms at three in the afternoon, so was given my current dose of 16 milligrams, sent home with Cloni-dine and Naproxone.

I am now sitting on my couch alone, my wife in Miami. Inside of me I can feel a terror growing. I don't know what to do. I listened to Nina Simone and cried. I listened to Stevie Nicks and cried. I wrote messages to far too many people knowing I wouldn't respond. I am lonely and feel as if I've had an organ removed.

My fear is that I do not know who I am. Being a dedicated drug addict, I did not miss a single day without opiates from the age of sixteen to the age of forty-three, save the time I was in rehab—but even in rehab I was taking prescribed Morphine. This is the first time since my pubic hair numbered in the single digits that I do not have *real* opiates (real meaning abusable), coursing through my system. I think heroin felt right because it slowed my brain down. My brain has been overactive since I splashed out of my mother into the end of the Vietnam War. I also found out recently that I have Borderline Personality Disorder, not Bipolar Disorder as I'd thought, so am taking 250 mg a day of Lamotrigine. This is supposed to help me with 'emotional regulation', but I suspect it will also make me stupid, as my unregulated emotions have been the source of much of my creativity.

Take the piano away from the pianist and what do you have? An asshole with too much time on his hands. I've always been an asshole with too much time on my hands, so if I double, or triple that time—time opiates slowed down—what will I be? Am I as smart as I've thought I am? Am I smarter? Dumber? Will I get fat, will I get boring, will I stop being funny, will my brain become a Broadway orchestra of obsessive thoughts? Will I attempt trepanning myself to send the horns and tap dancers into the clouds?

I fear all of it. Each option based on an altered self terrifies me. But I have no choice to wait and see who shows up to take the place of Brad Phillips.

There is worse. Something I try not to consider.

A roaring, gun grey fist of no-change, hammering me throughout the rest of my days.

3.

Likely 2012

well the last year basically i don't remember. I fired my psychiatrist i think when lee kicked me out. and then i wasn't accountable to anyone. i lived in the studio above her shop for a while and it was very dark and bad for me. the bathtub was only three feet long, the ceiling five feet high, and well you can see how tall i am. there was just a cot and a space to do my work and a pack of dusty cd's and a small bathroom and that's it and i lived there and i could hear her downstairs but she never came up. well maybe half a dozen times to yell at me. and in the day i usually just sat in the metropole on abbot and i was a regular and i mean in a really pathetic pitiful way and i was there from 11 to 5 or 6 because it was quiet, then when people started coming in i either went to really unsafe dive bars or the liquor store and i walked down alleys in the rain or sat on benches or curbs in the rain drinking or i sat in the park near the studio drinking. sometimes i would go to AA meetings but always got drunk after and i was often drunk when i got there and in fact would chair the meeting drunk. my doctor and other people including lee would say i was drunk and they could smell it and i would just refuse to admit it and make up ridiculous lies and know they didn't believe any of it. which, this is counter to my past because i was always so good at lying and no one ever suspected i was lying but it's the alcohol because it fucking smells and there's no way around that. before she kicked me out i'd have 5 baths a day and she still knew i think. she'd often call the house and she never knew where i was. i would go out and drink 5 doubles, come home and have a bath, go back and drink four pints and three shots, come home and have a bath. i'd never been cleaner and never been filthier. when i was still living with her. and it worked somehow. i mean i was coherent. mostly. we ate dinners i think. but at the end i would say i was going to the store and she basically said you're going to buy booze and i'd say no but of course i was and i came back after an hour and she'd smell it and i'd lie and it was so fucking humiliating and i was ashamed of my treating her that way. anyway she had enough of that so the studio is where i ended up. a month after my show, which put a bunch of money in my pocket. but it was untenable there, i remember once i looked at the toilet and realized that, from the appearance of it, I'd taken a giant shit on the back of the lid above the bowl sometime while i was in a blackout and it had hardened and stayed there. i had all this money from the canada council grant and some sales. so i was good to go mostly. but the studio was no good and in the end i was hanging out with this dealer named jay mostly and he had a place on hastings and a lot of times i'd just crash with him and i guess ended up living with him. which, he was a good guy but crazy, and at the bar he'd just pay for everything because dope dealers are lonely but we liked the same music and had the same style so we hung. we got drunk and bought live fish at t&t and put them in tourists backpacks. at his place i'd just snort the fattest fucking lines of mdma non-stop and it never fucked me up properly and he let me eat all his ecstasy and that was getting a bit fucked too because at some point I'd take maybe 14 of them and they still didn't work. or sometimes it worked because we'd be in the apartment full of dope with like a dozen or more stolen mountain bikes watching tv in the dark and i'd also be eating mushrooms like they were fucking olives and when we had to go out for smokes then yeah the ecstasy was working and i was fucked out of my mind like i didn't know what limbs were for and my eyes felt like globes and everything was light. anyway that lasted a while then this dude from the AA meeting i went to on a regular basis told me he had a room in his house and i took it and i shared it with this fucking psychotic possibly serially raping piece of shit monster who had like sixteen months clean but lost 5k a day gambling and got his dick sucked by the most desperate crack addicted hookers for ten bucks all day long and told me i had to get my shit together. the other guy was a good guy but he was barely hanging on to his sobriety and had two older daughters and was going back to school to have a real life again. he was someone i admired and he was trying to help me. but of course i couldn't stop and i worked some job for i can't remember how long, a temp job, and i made 9 bucks an hour and took a smoke break every half hour and during those breaks drank 5 double bourbons at the bar across the street where i was immediately a regular so i'd say i was probably spending 8 times what i was making to be at this fucking awful job but at least it got me out of the house and the alleys. for dinner i'd go to the worst italian place on hastings every single night and order the lasagna to go because while she heated it up i could drink maybe four bourbons and even though she loved me and i called her lucy she really overpriced her drinks and never cut me a break, and then i'd eat half the lasagna in my room maybe pass out in it and often have it in my beard or on my sweater when i woke up. and like these guys knew i was using and drinking and i was never remembering coming home and coming home with broken parts of my body and cuts and black eyes and basically they just turned a blind eye to it. i don't know why but they did. and i went to counseling sometimes with lee and i'd be loaded and she'd say it right there in the session and so would the doctor they'd both look at me in this small room where i'd be wearing a disgusting beige jacket that must have reeked of smokes and booze and ask me if i was drunk or high and i'd very articulately say no and really just get my back up. and i was way up on my clonazepam from 1mg a day to 8mg cause my psychiatrist i'd fired was a burnout and my GP had kept that super high dosage in my file. none of these doctors paid attention because they all thought i'd be dead any day so i'm doing all this with a pound and a half of clonazepam in me and eventually i just don't remember a fucking thing. i can remember sounds of broken glass. i can remember my forehead being slammed against pavement. i can remember so much vomiting in alleys, vomiting blood, throwing bottles, a paramedic saying i'd burned a hole in my esophagus. i can remember glimpses of fucking people i'd never have fucked, i can remember colours, seasons changing, but that's about it. then i went to the detox once cause lee saw i was fucked and suddenly remembered we were married and told them i needed help so i went. and i was so so sick and in paper slippers and pajamas all day and i couldn't smoke but it felt like home or at least a rest and i didn't know how to get out or if i wanted to get out and i remember i talked to my mom on the phone and i felt how i loved her so much. and there were identical twins in there crystal and lindsay and one was a junkie and one was a crackhead and i fucked the junkie one under a blanket in the group room before curfew while we watched that movie with robert downey jr. about charlie chaplin. she had a fat lip and whispered you wanna tie me up and i looked over and her twin sister gave me a thumbs up. lee came a few times and tried to play scrabble with her face twisted into the most disturbing rictus of a smile i'd ever seen and in her eyes i saw that i was gone forever to her. so after seven days in detox i took a cab to the ivanhoe two blocks away had a triple gin and tonic and went right back to it. it was summer. i don't remember where I was living to be honest. i remember going to a crime addicts anonymous meeting to get keys to somewhere and a dude said he was powerless over doing break and enters and i called bullshit on that in my head. i was a zombie on the downtown east side and i stayed in hotel rooms and in the beds of strangers, on the beach and in underground parking lots. and i fucked a rich girl named tiana from luxembourg who was maybe 20 years old in the bathroom of an after-hours and her face started going blue then her eyes rolled up and i slapped her as hard as i could and she sucked in air and then we left and we slept in a vacant lot off gore street that was a bog they'd filled with foam in the eighties.

ACKNOWLEDGEMENTS

Thank you Cristine Brache & Giancarlo DiTrapano.

Thank you to my editor Jordan Castro.

Thank you Andrew Berardini, Aaron Carpenter, Winnie H., Chelsea Hodson, Jay Isaac, Kay Kasparhauser, Catherine Millet, Sarah Nicole Prickett, Jeremy Riley, Dae Jong Sa, Brendan Sheppard-Missett, Lauren Smythe, Frances Stark, Sundance, Together We Can, and The City of Vancouver.

Brad Phillips is a writer and artist based in Scarborough, Ontario